SEXY BEAST

GEORGIA LE CARRE

ALSO BY GEORGIA

The Billionaire Banker Series

Owned
42 Days
Besotted
Seduce Me
Love's Sacrifice

Masquerade

Pretty Wicked
(Novella)

Disfigured Love

Crystal Jake
(The EDEN Series)

Click on the link below to receive news of my latest releases, fabulous giveaways, and exclusive content.
http://bit.ly/1Oe9WdE

—

Cover Designer:
http://www.bookcoverbydesign.co.uk/
Editor: http:// jlynnemorrison@hotmail.com/
Proofreader: http:// http://nicolarheadediting.com/

Sexy Beast

Published by Georgia Le Carre
Copyright © 2015 by Georgia Le Carre

ISBN: 978-1-910575-14-7

You can discover more information about Georgia Le
Carre and future releases here.

https://www.facebook.com/georgia.lecarre
https://twitter.com/georgiaLeCarre
http://www.goodreads.com/GeorgiaLeCarre

The Mouse On The Bar Room Floor

Some Guinness was spilt on the bar
room floor
When the pub was shut for the night.
Out of his hole crept a wee brown
mouse
And, in the pale moonlight,
He lapped up the frothy brew from the
floor,
Then back on his haunches he sat.
And all night long you could hear him
roar,
'Bring on the goddamn cat!'
—An Irish Tall Tale

Contents

ONE

Layla

Love is when a girl puts on perfume and a
boy puts on shaving cologne and they go out
and smell each other.

—Karl, Age 5

'**W**hat are you standing there for? Go
use the upstairs bathroom,' Ria says when
she spots me at the end of the queue for the
downstairs bathroom.

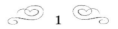

She is right. The queue *is* long. 'I'll just use the portaloo outside,' I reply.

'Don't be so silly. There's a humongous queue there, too.'

I bite my lip. Ria is BJ Pilkington's second cousin and we are in his house, Silver Lee, a cavernous mansion built in the art deco style with massive windows that wrapped all the way around the front and sides. BJ threw this party for my brother, Jake, and his new wife, Lily. And while I like and socialize with Ria, BJ and I share a stinging mutual dislike for each other.

In fact, I hadn't even wanted to come, but my mother forced me to. 'It's in your brother's honor,' she said in that displeased tone I knew not to disobey. 'It'd be ignorant not to, and God help me, I didn't bring you up to be ignorant.'

'Are you really sure it'll be OK?' I ask, looking doubtfully up the long, curving, dark wood staircase. Nobody else seemed to be going up it. It is understood that the party is restricted to the four reception rooms downstairs.

'Of course,' she insists confidently.

I give it one last attempt. 'I don't even know where it is, and I don't really want to go wandering around by myself.'

'Come on, I'll show you,' she says and, taking my hand, makes for the stairs.

'Thanks, Ria,' I concede, following her meekly. I do need the bathroom rather badly. At the top of the stairs I look down

and see all the beautiful people dressed in their absolute finest. That's the thing about us travelers. We love our color. Peacocks, all of us. There isn't a plain black gown in sight. Ria takes me down a corridor and half-opens a door to a blue and white bathroom.

'See you downstairs,' she calls cheerfully and walks away.

I use the toilet, then wash my hands and stand in front of the mirror. My deep auburn hair comes down to the tips of my breasts. My eyebrows are straight and my eyes are dark blue. My nose is narrow, my lips are generous, and my jaw is well defined.

I am wearing a duck egg blue taffeta dress that I designed and sewed myself. It has a tight bodice and a wide bow at the base of my spine, the ends of which trail lower than the hem of my mid-thigh, Honey Boo Boo-style skirt. Underneath are layers upon layers of gathered electric blue tulle and lace petticoats. Crinolines, my grandma used to call them.

I fluff them up. I love petticoats. In my opinion, life is way too short not to wear petticoats that stick out from under your skirt. I reapply my lipstick, press my lips, and leave the bathroom.

The corridor outside is deserted. Faint sounds of the party downstairs float up. As I walk down the carpeted passage I am suddenly and very strangely overcome by an irresistible curiosity. I want to open a door, just one, and see how BJ lives. I don't know why, since I think him an arrogant beast. But just for those seconds, I want to see more than what everyone downstairs will see.

Oh! What the hell, just a quick look.

I open a door. The interior is plain; it's obviously just a spare bedroom. I close it and open another. It, too, has an unlived-in appearance. Again, very plain. I try another door. It is locked. Okay, one last door and I'm out of here. I stop before another door handle and turn it.

Whoa!

BJ!

I take a step forward, close the door behind me, and lean against it. And fuckin' stare. Two rooms must have been merged into one to make such a massive space. The walls are black and the words 'No Fear' are painted in white using a large calligraphy font. They glow in the light from a real fire roaring in the fireplace. It's been a long time since I've seen real logs.

A large chandelier hangs from an iron hook in the ceiling; it looks more like a meat hook than a decorative accent. The bed is a huge, wrought iron four-poster, obviously custom, with deep red fleur-de-lis patterned brocade curtains that have been gathered and held together by thick gold and black ties. On the bedside tables that flank it are elaborate candelabras with real candles that have dripped wax onto the gilt handles.

Wow! So this is what lies inside BJ. His cold, cold eyes hide the soul of a seventeenth-century lord. It is dark and dangerous but I am strangely drawn to it. With some shock I realize that there is something irresistibly seductive about my discovery. It's like walking into BJ's private world or looking into his soul.

I try to imagine the room with the candelabras lit. The candlelight dancing off the walls. My eyes move to the bed and I see me naked and crushed under BJ's large, powerful body, the light making his muscles gleam. The image is so erotic; it is at once thrilling and disturbing. I feel a flutter in my tummy.

I frown. I hate the man. And that is putting it politely.

And yet, here I am in his bedroom. A place I should never be. But, still unwilling to leave, I walk to the middle of the room, my petticoats rustling, the heels of my shoes loud and echoing on the hardwood floor. The fire crackles. It feels as if I am in a different world. Like Alice in her wonderland.

As if pulled by invisible hands, I head toward an antique, dark oak dresser. In a trance I stroke the metal handle. It is cool, smooth, full of all the events it has seen for hundreds of years, the squabbles, the trysts. A frisson of strange excitement runs over my skin. I pull at the metal handle. The

drawer glides open with a whisper, smoothly, like it is on roller blades.

I stare wide-eyed at the contents.

Velvet boxes. Piled on top of one another. So many secrets. BJ's secrets. I take one and open it. A tiepin with a blue stone glitters up at me. I open another. A tiepin with a black panther, obviously old. I open another box and freeze. A gold tiepin that reads 'Layla' in cursive writing lays there. It ends with a small diamond at the end of it. I lift my head and look at the mirror above the dresser. I look different, strange, shocked. I shouldn't be here. This is wrong. I look into my eyes.

What the fuck are you doing, Layla?

But I don't turn away and run out of the room like any sane person would. Instead, I do a truly strange thing. Something I have *never* done before. I feel the blood pounding in my ears. So loud I cannot hear the logs crackling anymore. I take the tiepin out of its box, open my purse, and... oops... it falls in. Freaking strange that! I am a good girl, brought up as a proper Catholic. I don't take what's not mine. But my fingers snap my purse shut. The sound is loud and makes me jump. I can hear other sounds now, the merry fire and, faintly, the sounds of the party downstairs.

Slowly, almost afraid of what I will see, I raise my head and look at my reflection again. What I see there is far more

frightening than a thief. My reflection is no longer alone in the mirror. BJ is standing in the doorway. His huge, muscular body fills it entirely.

Oh God!

TWO

Layla

Cold fear races down my spine. My pulse accelerates wildly while my mind jerks into overdrive. Maybe he didn't see me lift his tiepin. Perhaps I could just slip past him. I could pretend I am lost and that I didn't realize I was in his *bedroom*. Maybe. Just maybe. Very deliberately, I place my forefinger on the edge of the drawer, shunt it closed, and turn around to face him. Some men have looks, others have charm. BJ has presence. An edgy, almost menacing presence. The moment he appears in a room he owns it. He changes the atmosphere the way a grizzly coming into a room does.

He is wearing a silver hoop in his right ear, a black T-shirt, army surplus camouflage trousers, and combat boots. He is half-pirate, half-smuggler. He remains perfectly still. Danger and power ooze out of him. My heart starts to hammer inside my chest. *I can do this,* I think defiantly. *I'm not scared of you. I'm an Eden. Edens eat Pilkingtons for breakfast.* Straightening my back and keeping my expression cool, I begin to walk toward him. I pray he cannot see my legs wobbling.

When I am five feet away I see his eyes. They are pools of gleaming black tar. No light there. They are flat and utterly impenetrable. For a fraction of a second I have the strangest impression of sexual tension. But of course, that is a trick of my overwhelmed emotions. His mouth is set in a forbidding line. I have seen it stretched in laughter, but never full on. Always from afar, by accident, and only from the corners of my eyes.

A foot away from his looming form I stop. He really is so damn huge. The scar on the top of his left cheek appears alive in the firelight. I swear no man has ever looked more inhospitable, or made me feel more intimidated.

'Sorry,' I say tightly. 'I got lost and wandered in here by mistake. I guess I better get back to the party.'

He does not step aside to let me through. He is so big, so meaty. He is like a predatory animal.

I clench my handbag tensely. 'Will you please move?'

'You want to pass? Squeeze past,' he suggests mildly, his face devoid of any expression.

'How dare you? I'll call my brother,' I threaten. Attack is always the best form of defense.

Something flashes in his eyes. I know then that I've made a mistake. I should have been more humble. It would have made my escape easier. He slips his large hand into his trouser pocket and produces a phone.

'That's a good idea.' His voice is silky with warning. 'Call him. Last time I looked he was with his pregnant wife. I believe your mother was sitting nearby, too. They can all rush up here to *my* bedroom and save their precious little princess.'

'What the hell is wrong with you?' I ask contemptuously.

His eyebrows rise. 'What the hell is wrong with me? You're a thief, Layla Eden.'

My cheeks flame, but I am not giving up so easily. 'I'm not,' I cry hotly.

'Then you have nothing to fear. Call your brother,' he invites.

I bite my lip. 'Look. I'm sorry I was in your bedroom. I'll just go downstairs and we won't spoil anybody else's night, OK?'

'OK.'

My mouth drops open at my effortless victory. I close it shut. 'Thank you,' I say softly and add a smile of gratitude.

'After you admit that you stole and ... I've punished you.'

A bark of incredulity explodes out of my mouth. 'What?'

'It's only fair. You make a mistake, you pay for it.'

My eyes narrow suspiciously. I knew it. I've always known it. He is no friend of our family. This is the proof I have been looking for—that he is just low, low, low. He has always been low and he will always be low. Enough even to blackmail me! Perhaps he wants me to reveal some of Jake's business secrets. 'What kind of punishment are you talking about?'

'You should have what you've never had ... a spanking.' His tone is terrifyingly pleasant.

I stare at him in disbelief. The idea is too ridiculous to contemplate. I laugh.

He doesn't. 'I fail to see the comedy.'

The laugh dies in my throat. 'You can't seriously mean to spank me?' I ask incredulously. I feel a chill invade my body.

He raises a challenging eyebrow.

'You seriously mean to spank me.' I repeat stupidly.

'The problem with you, Layla Eden, is that you were spoiled when you were young. Your Da and Jake were much too much in love with you to exercise any kind of discipline over you. As a consequence, you've grown up an unruly weed,' he explains patiently.

'How dare you—?' I begin.

But he interrupts me coldly. 'This is getting boring. The choice is simple: you apologize and submit to a spanking or we call your brother—or, if you prefer, your mother.'

Jake? My mother? My pseudo fury drains out of me like water from a sink plug. I worry my bottom lip and imagine my mother's eyes dimming with humiliation, Jake staring at me without comprehension. He has given me the best of everything. When we were young and poor, my mother says Jake would always forgo his share of something if I wanted it.

My actions are inexcusable. I have thoroughly disgraced and dishonored my family. I walked into a Pilkington's bedroom and stole something from it like a common thief. Worse of all, I have no idea why I did it. I've never done anything like this before. It is the stupidest, maddest thing I have ever done.

My gaze slides to his hands. They are as large as spades! My eyes jerk up to his tanned face. 'Why do you want to do this?'

He shrugs, nonchalantly, his face giving nothing away.

'There's nothing in it for you,' I insist desperately.

He smiles, an action devoid of any amusement. 'How do you know what's in it for me?'

My stomach sinks. I look at the space between his legs. It would be undignified, but I could try diving through it. I think I could make it, but it is almost certain that he will catch me, and that would be worse.

'Look,' I try to reason. 'I'm really, really sorry I came in here. It was wrong of me to intrude on your privacy, but if you let me go now I promise I won't tell a soul about any of this.' I wave my hand at the room. 'It'll be our secret.'

'That's a very kind offer, but I'm afraid there are only two ways you're leaving this room. With a spanking or,' he holds out his mobile phone in the middle of a baseball-mitt sized palm, 'or in your brother's company.'

I stare at the plain black phone. Physical punishment for me, or mental anguish for both Ma and Jake. Not much of a choice. I swallow hard and meet his eyes. 'I'll,' I whisper, 'take the ... punishment.'

'Great,' he says softly, slipping his mobile into his trouser pocket and taking a step forward. Suddenly the room seems so much smaller. Instinctively, I take a corresponding step backwards. He kicks the door shut with his heel.

'How do we do this?' My voice is clear and matter-of-fact. I have to assert some sort of control.

'I'll sit on the bed and you will position yourself on my lap. I will raise your skirt and spank you. Eight times.'

Raise my skirt! My eyes stray to his right hand. God! I feel heat creep over my body. Oh, the shame of it. And yet, to my absolute horror, there is something else sizzling in my core, something dark and hot. Something I'd never dreamed would happen to me. How could I be turned on by such a depraved, dreadful prospect? I look into his eyes. They are blank mirrors. There is nothing to see, only what I am. A thief.

But as I stare into his eyes, I see a flash of something old.

And suddenly I know. This humiliation is not punishment because I came into his bedroom and stole his tiepin. It is because of what happened when I was thirteen years old, when I tripped over a tree root and fell down. My skirt flew up and my panties showed. I can remember them even now, white cotton with red polka dots. All the other kids and BJ saw them. I hated everyone seeing them. I wanted to jump up, but I was too winded to move. Utterly humiliated and ashamed, I remained sprawled on the ground, an object of ridicule.

Some of the kids laughed. I knew them. They were afraid of Jake and they would never have dared laugh if BJ hadn't been there. At that time our families—BJ's and mine—were in a bitter generational feud. It is only recently that Jake and BJ had uprooted the barbed fences between our families. Since everybody knew about the bad blood, they thought they could ingratiate themselves with BJ by laughing at me.

But in a flash, BJ came to me and pulled me up easily. Even then he was a big lad. The other kids immediately ceased laughing. They were scared of him.

'Are you all right?' he'd asked.

But I was so mortally embarrassed that he had witnessed my humiliation, I lashed out ungratefully. 'Take your dirty hands off me, you filthy Pilkington, you,' I spat.

He had a mohawk then and it looked strange when he flushed bright red. He jerked his hand away from me.

I turned on my heel huffily, and limped away on my twisted ankle, my nose held high. I knew he was watching me but I didn't give him the satisfaction of turning back to look. After that we became enemies. And now he had caught me in his bedroom.

Finally, he can exact his revenge.

He takes a step towards me and I nearly cower, but he only strides past me. Alarm plucking at my belly, I watch him sit

on his enormous bed, slap his thigh and say, 'Ready when you are.'

'Where force is necessary, there it must be applied boldly, decisively and completely. But one must know the limitation of force; one must know when to blend force with a maneuver, a blow with an agreement.'

—Leon Trotsky 1879 -1940

THREE

Layla

He holds a hand out to me. Dazed with disbelief, I walk up to him. Even now, I still can't believe he means to go through with it. This surely must be the part where he admits it has all been a brutish Pilkington joke. My eyes plead frantically with him.

'Lie across my lap,' he instructs politely.

Oh dear God! For a moment I cannot move, my mind unable to accept that he

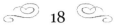

really expects me to submit to such humiliation.

Unaffected by my silent pleas, he cocks a dark eyebrow and nods meaningfully at his lap. 'No need to be shy. I've seen it all before, remember?' he taunts.

Our eyes lock. I flush furiously. Then my pride kicks in. *No, you despicable, disgusting, insufferable man, you haven't seen it all. So much has changed since you last looked.*

My bottom is naked, but for three bits of string and the smallest triangle of black lace. It's a far cry from the polka dot underwear he once saw. Only this morning, I had exfoliated my entire body until it was silky smooth, then rubbed Golden Brown Level 3 fake tan over every inch. I have nothing to be ashamed of. I am glowing!

I lift my chin and stare down at him with a mixture of contempt and stiff hatred. His reaction is to twist his lips with amusement.

I drop my purse to the floor and, gritting my teeth, I put my hand into his and gingerly lower myself onto his lap. I flinch when my skin makes contact with the steel-like muscles of his thighs. I turn in his hard lap and bend forward, laying my palms flat on the floor to steady myself. In order to keep my legs firmly together, my knees are straight and stiff. The tips of my toes don't touch the floor and hot blood floods into my head. The position is awkward and unsteady. My nose is less than a foot away from the dark floor and I can see the grain in the naked wood as it glows purple in the firelight.

'Are you ready?'

Hell would have to freeze over before I agree that I am.

Glad that my hair is hiding my burning face, I close my eyes with impotent fury and shame. He grasps the many layers of my skirt and flips them over my lower back ... and becomes completely still. So still it affects even the air in the room. A mad thrill runs through me. *You haven't seen it all have you, big guy?* Another thought: he's not immune.

I hear him inhale sharply before a large callused palm rests on the cheeks of my bottom. I know he can see the string of my panties between my pussy lips. Resentment races down my spine, but I am suddenly conscious that I am inexplicably wet. His palm is still resting on my skin. I feel it move slightly, almost a caress but not quite and I feel myself begin to tremble.

BJ

Who'd have fuckin' thought?

Layla Eden's damn near naked ass laid out like an eat-as-much-as-you-want banquet in *my* lap. I gaze down at my rough palm resting peacefully on her silky smooth skin in astonishment. Freaking unbelievable! How is this even possible? My cock gets busy inside my pants and I'm suddenly harder than I've been in my whole life. A state I'm clearly entitled to given the exceptional circumstances—I am, after all, looking down at Layla Eden's golden bottom sprawled across my fuckin' lap.

You got the peaches, I got the cream, babe.

The desire to caress the pert, round shape is so powerful, its pull catches me off guard. Lightly, almost against my will, my

hand brushes the smooth center of the twin globes of firm flesh. That almost imperceptible action makes her body jerk. A shocked 'oh' tumbles out of her full lips and her right arm lifts off the floor, sinking her balance. Suddenly it's panic at all stations, her body tilts precariously and her deliciously long legs start flailing.

With pleasure, my other hand wraps firmly around her waist. She has a wasp-like waist. I could span it with my hands. She returns her palm back to the floor and some semblance of order is restored.

I gaze down at my catch.

Her ass is a coy little thing, prudishly hiding her anus. Originally, there'd only been just enough of a gap underneath her cheeks to show off a tantalizing triangle of lace-curtained pussy, however since the pointless panic episode, her legs have moved further apart, and she is now quite brazenly exposing a fair bit of her fruitcake. Which, I must say, for a thin girl is surprisingly plump and ripe looking. Between the fat, pink lips, the black G-string of her panties is stretched tight and cutting rather cruelly into her flesh. Update: wet flesh. Someone is getting a little excited for her punishment, methinks.

It really is the most perfect sight.

Almost an open invitation.

My fingers itch to push aside the ridiculous string and enter her pussy. What would she do? Scream blue murder, no doubt. And that wouldn't be a bad thing. Hell, I'd love to fuck this woman spitting and hissing. I don't think I've ever been with such a haughty bitch before. Even the thought has me salivating, but I've got to pretend that this is about chastisement and not pleasure.

'You will count the blows or they will not register,' I tell her, my voice dead detached.

She freezes and around my palm gooseflesh begins to form on her perfect skin.

'Get on with it,' she grates.

I smile to myself. *Ah, Layla, you're so fuckin' transparent, so perfectly predictable.* She is determined to get through this unpleasant business as soon as possible and never give me the satisfaction of hearing her cry out.

No can do, baby.

I open my fingers on her butt and she tightens her cheeks with anticipation. I can't help it. My fingers curl and I squeeze the firm flesh. She moans and the unmistakable scent of her arousal hits me like a call during mating season. It's the kind of smell that can drive a man—well, me anyway— crazy. Heavy, suffocating, insistent. I want to answer it.

Layla Eden may be a snooty, spoilt bitch, but l want to fuck her so bad I'm like those dogs that jump fences and break their legs just because a bitch in heat is passing by on the other side. Hers is the kind of body that I can spend all night, every night, diving into. I want to pick her up like the doll she is, open her legs wide, and suck until her flavor runs over my tongue and coats my throat. Hours later, when she is passed out cold, I want to be able to swirl my tongue and taste her in my mouth all over again.

A voice in my head urges, *Jump the fence then. Break a leg. It'll heal. She bloody well asked for it. Didn't she come into your bedroom of her own freewill?* But another sane voice is already warning. *Even this is madness. What the fuck do you think you're doing with Jake's fuckin' sister?* I listen to the sane voice. I have resisted the call of her delicious body off and on over the years. I can do it again.

I could never really decide if I wanted to spank her saucy ass until it was scarlet or fuck her senseless. Now appears both impulses come from the same place. I watch her body. Frozen in place. Tense. Waiting for the flat of my hand.

I *will* hit her hard, hard enough to successfully convince her that this is a punishment and not the sexual encounter it is. I will be methodical. Each slap will land on a different spot. One cheek, then the other. Under the cups of flesh, and finally, where her thighs meet her body.

I rest the forearm of my left hand across her back and watch her toes curl. A

delightfully involuntary response. I raise my hand and hold it suspended high above my head. Ms. Eden's butt trembles helplessly.

Oh! Yes ...

FOUR

Layla

I have never been smacked or beaten in my life. By anyone. Ever. And as soon as the heat from his palm leaves my skin I experience a wild second of pure, unadulterated panic. With my heart pounding like a war drum, I squeeze my eyes shut and prepare myself for the blow, but nothing happens.

What seems like an age passes.

Just as I think he has changed his mind after all, and relief starts pouring into my body, I feel him pull away slightly and a subtle disturbance in the air above me as his palm hurtles through it.

Thwack! His hand, heavy and hard, lands on my flesh.

I make no sound at all. First, I am absolutely determined not to give this vile beast of a man the satisfaction of a reaction. Second, the blow does not immediately register as painful. But a moment later I feel the effect. My eyes widen and my mouth opens in a silent O. By God, that really hurt! Tears of mortification well up in my eyes. I have to squeeze my eyes closed to try and prevent them from dropping.

He pauses. 'I'm waiting for a number,' he reminds me casually.

A number? What a sadistic bastard. He has no heart, this man. A hot needle of hatred for my tormentor stabs through me. I open my mouth. Shockingly nothing comes out. I try again. A totally unrecognizable shallow gasp exits.

'One.'

Almost immediately his hand crashes again onto my skin, but this time I feel the searing pain straight away. Bravely, I suck in my breath. Other than calling out in a trembling voice, 'Two,' I make no sound to express the fiery agony I am in. I have never suffered such pain in my entire sheltered life.

Another blow slams down and I bite back a scream. Even though each stroke has hit a different place, they all serve to build on the existing burn. My bottom feels like it is on fire. I press my palms so hard into the floor to refrain from wriggling and squirming or covering my bottom that my knuckles show bone white.

'Three,' I croak hoarsely. I *hate, hate, hate* him. I never thought it was possible to hate someone this much. I am getting closer and closer to unstoppable tears.

The pitiless thrashing continues. The pain is now so intense I barely manage to call out, 'Four.' My butt screaming, I take shallow breaths. My hate has grown in direct proportion to the shame and pain he is forcing me to endure. Halfway there, I tell myself. And the thought is so disheartening I want to bawl my eyes out.

The fifth falls on the tender, fiery skin of the curve of my bottom and I feel as if I will die of pain. The sting is unbelievable. To my eternal humiliation, a howl slips out.

'Ooooowww.' At this point tears are freely running down my face; I am like a baby. I can't talk. I can't breathe.

'Call it out.'

'Five, you asshole, five,' I sob, all pretense and pride shattered.

BJ

The last imprint of my hand shows white for a second before it reddens to a deep pink to match the rest of her ass. There are still three strikes to go, but her defenses are already broken. She is sobbing openly, and I know that the next blow will elicit a full scream.

But that's not what I want.

Not at all.

My pelvis is brushing her beautifully reddened ass and my nose is filled with the smell of her. I am hot. My dick is like a hunk of wood straining against the zipper of my pants. I want to fuck her so bad. My hands itch to grab her by the hair, spread her thighs, and rip into her slippery little cunt so deep she hisses with pain and pleasure as her muscles flutter like crazy around my

dick. I want to empty my balls into her while she sees stars. Fuck, yeah.

But, of course, I don't.

This is Jake Eden's baby sister.

Instead ... I allow my little finger to spread out a little so it almost makes contact with her inner thighs, her sex. I rest my palm for a few seconds on her skin, my pinkie almost touching the glistening, salmon-colored flesh. The next time I raise my hand I will spank her pussy. Slowly, I lift my hand and let it hover in the air. Her tender skin is damp and glowing with sweat. Then I let the next wicked swing loose.

She shudders with shock and white-hot lust.

My little finger comes away wet. I smile with satisfaction. She freezes, her breathing shallow. I want to see her face. Very deliberately, I put both my hands on the bed on either side of me. Coldly, I say, 'I'm done.'

Immediately she scrambles to the floor and, crawling away, crouches like a cornered animal. She looks up at me with big, wet eyes full of hatred. Tears sparkle on her eyelashes. Her mouth quivers with temper. The princess exterior has been stripped away. Only the raw and helplessly sexual animal inside every human remains. Just as I know her buttocks must be humming, I know she will never admit that she is more turned on than she has ever been.

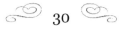

'Are you satisfied now, you sick bastard?' she spits. She is so furious her voice shakes.

'Fix your clothes and return to the party,' I tell her callously.

Using her palms to lever herself up, she springs to her feet and pulls her multi-layered skirts down over her stinging skin so roughly it makes her wince. She glares at me.

'I hate you,' she whispers.

'Join the queue.'

'I know now why they call you the bat. You're a fucking vampire, living in this ridiculous black dungeon.'

I shrug and look at her without expression. Sticks and stones maybe. Words? Forget it.

'I hope I never lay eyes on you again,' she hurls bitterly at me.

I watch her snatch her purse from the floor, and start walking towards the door.

'Layla.' My voice is a like whip. Even in her state she didn't dare disobey it.

She turns around and stares defiantly at me.

'My tiepin.'

She is so furious she very nearly breaks the clasp of her purse as she wrenches it open. She digs around, finds my tiepin, and violently flings it at my face.

I catch it easily in one hand. 'Enjoy the party,' I advise calmly.

'Pervert,' she snarls and slams the door shut on my mocking laughter. Sure, I get it: hers is the tale of the Princess and the Pea in reverse. She didn't enjoy being confronted with the animal inside her. Me, I am irredeemably base and animalistic, making me beyond excited to be acquainted with a newly created creature in my bedroom.

FIVE

Layla

The sounds of the party float up to me as I stand shocked and frozen in the hallway. Then it hits me: any moment now he could open the door and come out. With a panicked sob, I turn left and run for the bathroom. I lock the door with shaking fingers, and lean back against it, panting hard.

Why, oh why, did I ever go into his bedroom? Now *everything* is messed up. I

look in the mirror. A red-faced stranger with smeared make-up, a gaping mouth, and crazy eyes stares back. Anger and hate sparkle in my eyes, but there is something else too. Something more primal.

I drop my gaze hurriedly and turn on the tap, splashing cold water on my face. I feel hot, confused, angry, and ashamed. My bum is stinging like mad, but ... God, I feel alive, in a way I have never felt. And ... I am wet. So wet.

The primal look in my eyes is pure arousal.

Sexual excitement.

Jesus! Oh sweet Jesus. What the fuck is wrong with me? I cannot understand why I am aroused. I hate that son of a bitch. I've always hated him. He is a callous, uncouth man-whore. A sleazy, bag of shit who regularly sleeps with strippers and makes his money running sex clubs. He's practically a criminal. I abhor men like him. Even through the tears that had filled my eyes, I had seen the satisfaction and gloating triumph on his face.

I should be livid.

I *am* livid. The memory of his large palm, full of calluses landing on my bare buttocks fills my head. With that last strike he had deliberately slapped my, my unmentionables. He had allowed his dirty fingers to touch my sex! How dare he? Bastard!

I turn around, lift my skirt, and look back at my throbbing bottom in the mirror. It is lobster red. I feel the fury bubbling in my veins, but another sensation more powerful than anger intrudes. I don't want to examine or address it. Taking deep, calming breaths, I repair my make-up with trembling hands, then open the door and stick my head outside.

The hallway is deserted.

I start walking down it, but as I pass his bedroom door I start running. At the top of the stairs I stop and walk down the steps slowly. No one has missed me or seen anything. Everything is exactly as I left it and yet I'm entirely different. My hands won't stop trembling and there is a tight knot of tension in my stomach. All I want to do is run away. I will die if I have to see him again in the state I am in. I walk quickly towards the main room, my eyes darting around fearfully. Fortunately I spot my brother, Jake, standing head and shoulders above the crowd. The sight of him makes me want to start bawling. Squaring my shoulders I push through the crowd and go to him. He is looking down at Lily with a lovesick expression on his face.

'Jake,' I call, my voice tremulous.

His head whips around, his body is immediately tense and his eyes narrow dangerously. 'What is it?' he asks.

'I don't feel well. I want to go home. Can you call me a taxi?'

He takes a step towards me, his body relaxing with relief. He is over-protective I can't even begin to imagine what utter havoc would ensue if he knew what BJ has done to me.

He puts an arm around my shoulder lovingly. 'What's wrong, little bear?'

I want to throw my arms around him and cry my eyes out, but I don't. I bite back my tears and lean against his strong, warm body. 'I think I ate something that didn't agree with me. I've just been sick in the toilet,' I lie miserably.

'Come on, we'll take you home. Shane can give Ma a ride when she's ready to go.'

Lily comes forward, her eyes are concerned and she is playing along, but she is a woman and she does not believe my fairy tale.

'I'll go find BJ. I should tell him we are leaving.'

I clutch his hand with both of mine and look up at him pleadingly. 'Can't you just call him from the car and tell him?'

He looks as if he is about to say something, but thinks better of it, and nods. Then the three of us make our way to a smiling girl in a Playboy bunny costume who takes our tickets and gives us our coats. It is only when we get outside that I am able to breathe properly again. I hardly hear when Jake gets on the phone with BJ and then Shane to arrange Ma's ride home.

I am too bruised and shaken.

SIX

BJ

I stand at the curving windows with my back to the party and watch her leave, Jake's arm curved protectively around her narrow back. Something within the darkest recesses of me whirls loose and flaps noisily in the wind. I had managed to ignore it for this long, but I know I cannot secure it back the way it was. You could say that the old hand is back, knocking at the old door.

I don't open the door.

My fists clench tight. I'll find release in another body. It was only a base animalistic

reaction. There is nothing special about her. I'll find a body more suited to my taste and fuck it. A lush, full-figured woman. A pair of hips I can grab while I am ramming into her. Someone who won't look at me as if I have crawled out of the sewers, as if I make her feel itchy and unclean.

Yet my behavior was rotten. I shouldn't have given in to my crazy impulse. So unlike me and so fuckin' foolish.

I turn away from the window. The party is still in full swing, but it is as if all flavor has been sucked out of it. A hand lands on my arm. I look down at it. Oval-shaped nails painted pearlescent, good skin. I let my eyes flow upwards.

Mmmm ... tight, yellow dress clinging onto breasts like planets. Well, big enough to feed a small African tribe anyway. I like that. Abundance. That's what stuck-up, spoilt Layla lacks.

And blonde. Yeah. I'm *very* partial to blonde pussy.

My eyes rise higher up to a plump, slightly sulky mouth. Perfect for sucking cock.

By the time I reach her eyes, it's a done deal. Cornflower blue, of course. As pretty as flowers and no hint that she sees anything unclean or itchy about the view in front of her.

I vaguely recognize her. The memory is fuzzy, but I think she's candy from one of Shane's clubs. I sort of remember flirting

 38

with her at the party Jake threw to celebrate the reopening of Eden. However, if I remember correctly, I ended up leaving with another dancer. It occurs to me that I had seen Layla that night too, and she had been rude to me then too. Bitch.

'Hello,' Blondie drawls. 'You went home with the South American dancer the last time.'

I smile, letting it reach all the way up to my eyes. 'I might have been a bit drunk and my cock might have been waylaid around the corner from you.'

She leans closer. 'You're not drunk tonight, are you?'

'As sober as a saint.'

'Good. Cause my pussy's been aching for that great fuck you promised ever since.'

My smile widens. I could do with a dose of random cunt. There is comfort, immense comfort in anonymous curves. 'I remember you now. You're the one who can suck cock for days.'

She smiles with satisfaction that I have remembered her. 'That's right. I can suck cock like you can't believe.'

I grab Blondie and, swinging her around, walk her backwards until her back presses against the wall, and she is hidden from the room by my bulk. I slide my hand under her dress and she helpfully spreads her legs. She is not wearing panties. Perfect. My kind of girl. She moans as my fingers part her slippery folds. She is so wet, even I am impressed.

'What's this?' I ask.

'Tug it and see,' she suggests.

I tug at the metal stud in her pieced labia.

She wriggles and tilts her pelvis towards me.

I insert a finger into her and slowly fuck her with it.

'Harder,' she urges throatily.

I fit another two fingers in and pump her so roughly her body jerks.

'Yes, yes,' she encourages fiercely, her eyes glazed with lust.

She's great, but she won't be enough. Not tonight. Not when I am this wired. I've got too much energy to burn. She'll be out cold before I'm finished.

'Listen cupcake, I'm looking for a threesome tonight,' I whisper in her ear.

'I have a friend,' she gasps immediately.

'Good. Go get her.' I take my fingers out of her pussy and hold them in front of her mouth. She tilts her head forward and sucks them greedily the way she would a dick, while staring boldly into my eyes. Yup, *definitely* my kind of girl.

My fingers exit her mouth with a wet pop.

I step sideways to let her pass, and watch her truly round and wonderful ass samba as she goes off in search of another body for me. I feel rather pleased with myself. It's gonna be a goooooood night, after all.

I bring my hand up to my nose and smell it, but she has sucked away the smell of her pussy. All that is left is Layla's scent, lingering like a rare perfume from a lost garden.

Damn you, Layla Eden. Just damn you.

Her friend is a Rita Hayward look alike, but with flaming copper hair. Obviously another dancer; I can always tell by the confident way they move. Unlike women who don't use their bodies to earn money, dancers get that their physical form gives them immense power over mere men. She slides up to me sinuously. I swear I have never seen a woman to walk in such a serpentine fashion before. It is actually fascinating to watch. My cock twitches with interest.

'I have a thing for men with gleaming raven hair,' she says, stopping less than six inches away from me. The tips of her perky breasts almost touch my abs.

'Oh yeah?' Her obvious attraction is a balm after Layla's unconcealed contempt and disgust.

A knowing smile stretches across her scarlet lips. 'Yeah. Is it true what they say about you?'

'I don't know, what do they say?'

She lays her palms on my chest, stands on tiptoe, and whispers into the side of my neck. 'That your mama gave you a horse cock.'

I grin slowly.

She puts her hand on my hardening dick, rubs along the length of it through the material and slowly opens her mouth as if she is becoming unbearably sexually stimulated. It is a practiced but highly effective move.

'Oh! That's no horse cock. That's a whole python you have there in your jeans, Mister,' she teases with a sly smile.

Yeah, she'll do.

SEVEN

BJ

The party is still going strong but I know my housekeeper, Marcel, will see to throwing everybody out when he starts to miss his bed. With a hand resting lightly on the small of each girl's back, I herd them away from the party and up to the Green Room.

I throw open the door and they enter like frisky lambs to the slaughter. I close the door, hit a switch, and a rotating disco ball with hundreds of colored LEDs comes on. Multi-colored light scatters around the room. I flick another switch and rap music throbs to life, Jason Derulo and Snoop Dogg go, 'Wiggle, wiggle, wiggle.'

The Green Room is the ultimate in bad taste. It has a mirrored ceiling, the largest bed in Britain dressed up with black satin sheets, red embossed wallpaper, a glass-fronted fridge with all manner of drink, and an Aladdin's showcase of sexual toys. The girls squeal with delight. They know that when something is this fucking bad it has to be good.

'Want something to drink?' I ask.

'No thanks,' Rita says and Blondie giggles.

'Get naked then.'

They waste no time. Quickly and expertly they shimmy off the few garments they're wearing. Blondie has the better body, but Rita's ass makes my jaw hang. Her flaming copper pubes are trimmed into a heart over the top of her pussy and Blondie is freshly shaven, which kinda makes me think she isn't a real blonde. In my experience, real blondes generally leave something behind as their badge of authenticity.

As if one mind, the girls gambol over to the showcase of toys. Both know exactly what they want. Rita gets a strap on dildo and Blondie chooses a vibrator and a long leather belt. They walk over to the huge bed with their toys and crawl to the middle of it. Getting on their knees, they face each other.

Dappled light flows over their bodies, like they're creatures from an eighties porn flick.

Blondie leans in and pushes her tongue into Rita's mouth, her golden flesh pressing against Rita's pale skin as they deepen their kiss. Then Rita, obviously the stronger character of the two takes over. She breaks the kiss and with a coy glance at me, bends her head and begins sucking Blondie's red-tinted nipples. Blondie moans. Her hand moves downwards to finger Rita's pussy.

It's a cute show. Real cute. My cock hardens, but my heart remains utterly unmoved and cold. I stroll over to the fridge and get a bottle of beer, uncap it on the side of the fridge, take a swig, and turn around to watch the girls.

Rita falls away from Blondie. She lands on the bed on her back and spreads open her creamy alabaster thighs. Blondie immediately dives face first into her flaming muff and starts licking her out. Rita's pussy must be a juicy thing. From where I stand I can hear the wet sounds of Blondie slurping and licking while Rita mews with pleasure.

I concentrate on Blondie's beautiful ass. She has it stuck high in the air in a deliberately provocative way with her legs stretched far enough apart to give me a graphic view of her pussy. It's fucking beautiful. All baby pink and luscious. The stud catches the light and glitters. She bobs her hips suggestively to make it obvious that she is inviting me to fuck her.

I smile inwardly. As if I need an invitation. This is my show, babe.

Then, all of a sudden, unexpectedly and for no good reason I can think of, a black string rudely separating Layla's salmon-colored folds flashes into my mind. And I remember the heady private smell of her that made me fantasize about grabbing her by the waist and dropping her on my upright dick. The craving to see her securely impaled on my dick had been almost overpowering. Not even Blondie and Rita together could bring forth such an overpowering desire. The thought irritates me.

I'm fucking invincible. I have no chinks in my armor. None.

And I don't need no stuck-up princess in my life.

I put the bottle on the top of the fridge, undress and stroke my throbbing length as I walk over to the side table. I take out a condom and roll it over my length. I see both Blondie's and Rita's eyes excitedly swivel in their heads to watch my inked body and my horse cock.

I kneel on the bed, grab Blondie by her full round hips and fucking bury myself so deep inside her, her head pulls back violently and her shocked mouth emits a strangled cry. Rita's hands grab Blondie by the hair to guide her mouth back onto her shiny pussy.

I pause. 'Too hard?'

'No. She likes it rough,' Rita says quickly.

Full of Rita's pussy, Blondie nods her agreement.

That is all I need.

Like a jackhammer I pump my cock balls-deep into Blondie. Her whole body jerks with the force of my thrusts even if her cries are muffled against Rita's snatch. We keep this up even while Rita climaxes with a howl to wake up the dead. Blondie's job is clear. It's licking up Rita's juices until Rita says otherwise.

One final slam and I explode with a great roar.

I pull out of Blondie's swollen, thoroughly fucked pussy and immediately Rita's voice rings out, 'Suck him.'

No rest for the wicked.

Blondie immediately makes a hundred and eighty degree turn on her hands and knees, her pendulous breasts bouncing. With admirable expertise she peels the condom off my dick with her lips and tongue. Opening her mouth, she takes my semi-hard cock deep into her warm velvety mouth. As she begins the task of sucking it into a full erection, I knot the used rubber and fling it over my shoulder.

Meanwhile, Rita ties on the strap on dildo and roughly plunges it into Blondie.

Rita is so brutal I almost feel sorry for Blondie. Although, to give Blondie her due, she never complains or attempts to dislodge my growing dick from her mouth. The bigger I become, the more impressed I become with Blondie's dedication and skill. Fuck, with Rita slamming into her, I am so deep inside her throat my balls are pressed into her chin, but the girl doesn't even exhibit a gag reflex.

Instead, incredibly, she is not only moving back and forth along my length, she is also slowly moving her tongue from side to side underneath my dick. It's like a deeply satisfying and completely sensuous massage. Frothy white streams of pre-cum and spit gather at the corners of her mouth and dribble down her neck.

I throw my head back and look up at the mirror.

It's fun to watch my dick disappear so completely into a pretty face and I dig the sight our bodies make in the mirror overhead. I am face-fucking Blondie while Rita batters Blondie's poor pussy. With a grunt of satisfaction I shoot my load directly into Blondie's stomach.

EIGHT

BJ

I withdraw from her mouth and walk over to the fridge. After a swig of flat beer, I turn back to watch them. Rita is relentlessly hammering into Blondie. Sure looks like Blondie has picked the short straw. Rita has climaxed, I have come twice, and Blondie has had nothing. I walk over to the bed to pull Blondie off the dildo and open her legs. Shit, her pussy is really red and swollen. I lick it gently.

'Don't let her come,' Rita says.

49

Blondie's eyes become huge. 'Let me come. Please.'

'You can come whenever you want to,' I tell her, with an edge to my voice.

I put my lips around her clit and suck gently. She comes explosively almost immediately.

Sucking her has made me hard again. I lie on my back and Rita, who has discarded her strap on, fits a condom on my dick and climbs on top of me. Angling my cock to her core she pushes herself down. Her pussy is tighter than Blondie's and it closes around me like a perfectly-fitted glove. I groan from the heat and snugness.

'Fuck,' she groans. 'You're so big it's like fucking a bloody baguette.'

That said, she begins to ride me slowly and deliberately. As soon as she judges that she can comfortably take all of me she begins to slam herself down on my cock. Her orgasm comes quickly, but it lasts a long time. Panting hard she rises off me and Blondie gets on.

'I want to suck your tits,' I tell her and immediately she pushes her full breasts forward. I grasp them both in my hands, squeezing them together so I can suck both her nipples at the same time.

'Harder,' she begs.

Now I know why Rita was being deliberately rough with her. Blondie gets off on pain. I bite her nipples until she cries out.

'Want me to stop?' I ask.

'No,' she moans. 'Suck me until I am so swollen and raw even wearing my dress again will be painful.'

And that is exactly what I do. I suck them hard enough for her to be in constant pain while she fucks herself on me and brings herself to another orgasm.

'Demi loves to have her ass spanked ... hard,' Rita tells me with that sly, almost evil smile of hers, her lips still glossy with my cum.

I look at Blondie/Demi. Her eyes are shining eagerly.

My mind flashes to Layla. This is turning to be a strange night. Fuck, the last thing I want to do is spank anyone else. Still...

'Use your belt,' Rita urges.

Blondie scrambles out of bed and brings the belt to me. 'Let me have it,' she begs. I take the belt from Blondie and she quickly goes and buries her face between Rita's legs while her ass hovers tantalizingly in the air.

'She'll suck me while you punish her,' she says excitedly.

I hold the belt in my fist and take the first swing. An angry red stripe blooms right across the middle of Blondie's fair skin. She grunts, but carries on slurping Rita's pussy. Rita nods in approval and wraps her legs around Blondie's head.

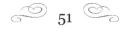

Blondie wriggles her bum to indicate her approval of the situation. So I let her have some more. Her plump bottom and the backs of her thighs turn a brilliant scarlet and Rita groans with pleasure, but suddenly, I find myself starting to tire of their game. I want to bring it to a close.

'Widen your legs,' I order.

Blondie rushes to obey.

I swing the leather right on her clit. She screams and climaxes instantly. Totally spent, she falls to one side. She is already snoring gently when I grab Rita and shove my never-ending erection into her mouth. She sucks on it willingly and voraciously, but it is not enough. For some reason I feel angry. With her. With myself. With the entire world. I grab a fistful of her hair and holding her head still, fuck her mouth hard and fast, but it is still not enough.

I pull out of her and push her so she is flat on her back.

I order her to raise her hips and she obeys immediately. While pinching her nipple I shove a finger into her ass. As I finger fuck her ass I tell her to do the same to her pussy. She does two things. She squeezes my finger with her ass and plunges two fingers into her gaping hole again and again until she squirts all over her own hand. Drops of dew glisten on her coppery, heart-shaped pubic hair.

'I cannot tell you how much I enjoyed your performance,' she whispers, her eyes

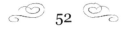

sultry, her forefinger delicately tracing the ink on my forearm. She looks at me with a wheedling expression. God, I detest women who pretend to be weak in order to control men.

I immediately start moving away from her.

'Fuck Demi in the ass before you go,' she says suddenly, her voice hard as pebbles.

I turn around and look at her. She is smiling, but her eyes are fathomless pits of shadows. For an extraordinary moment something shimmers between us, her cruelty, my coldness.

My cock stirs to life.

I turn my head to look at the sleeping girl. She is lying on her side with her knees curled. Poor thing can't sleep on her front because her nipples are so raw they are twice their natural size. Can't sleep on her back because her ass is so angry. Even her pussy has been so battered it juts out like a peeled plum from between her thighs. It actually looks as sore as hell.

I turn back to Rita and her eyes are an open door into the darkness in her soul. At that moment I see into her. And suddenly I pity her ... and myself.

Is this it for us?

Is this all, we who save ourselves above everyone else, and thrive at the expense of others, will ever have?

Anonymous, meaningless fucks with other damaged creatures of the night. Where there is no guilt because it is too dark to see the willful damage we leave behind. At moments like this, does a little part of my soul crumble into dust, and fly away? The secret to the labyrinth is always at the beginning. Before you enter. Once you do it is too late. The thought makes me feel empty and depressed.

'Breakfast is included,' I say coldly, as I vault off the bed.

'Is sausage on the menu?' she calls.

I don't answer her. Naked, I head for the shower. My hands are not clean. My greatest enemy is myself.

NINE

Layla

I walk into my local supermarket, pick up a basket, and head towards the milk section, where I grab a carton. I then quickly make for the yogurt shelves. I haven't told anyone, not even Madison, my best friend, about the disgraceful thing I did in BJ's bedroom two weeks ago, or the way he retaliated. It is a combination of confusion and shame. Specifically, my reaction to the punishment I received. Sometimes, at night when I am in bed, it pops into my mind and I quickly kick it away without examining it.

It seems to fit in with the tawdry mess that my life has disintegrated into. Only a month ago my life seemed perfect. I had a gorgeous boyfriend, I was training as an apprentice at a top interior design firm in Milan (a post Jake had secured for me), and I was feeling strong and independent. Then last month I walked out of my job without telling anyone and ran back home with my tail between my legs. It all began when I opened a little email that began with

You are fucking MY boyfriend!

When it's in Italian it sounds a lot worse. She had attached hundreds of photos going back five years, which indeed proved that I was fucking her boyfriend. They had celebrated birthdays, barbeques, parties, and countless occasions in the company of a whole crowd of friends, none of whom I had met, of course.

I sat at my desk utterly shocked and sick to my stomach.

But he told me I was the most beautiful woman he had ever met. That no one was more beautiful than me. And he was going to take me to meet his parents next week!

I stayed over in his apartment. There had been nothing to tell me that he was cheating and so blatantly. There wasn't even

a case of lipstick in his bathroom cupboard. The magnitude of his deception was inconceivable. Unbelievable.

I looked at his handsome face in the pictures laughing, happy, and utterly devoted to the pretty, olive-skinned woman at his side. I hadn't known him at all. Or was it simply that I was more naïve that even my brothers believed? I felt so stupid. So cheated. So hurt. I didn't want anyone to know that I had been the victim of such an elaborate charade and I *never* wanted to see the slick bastard again. All I wanted to do was run home to my mother's house and lick my wounds in private.

Since he was one of the top designers in the firm, I simply dropped my belongings into a plastic bag and left without telling anyone. I went back to my apartment, packed my bags, and caught a business flight back to London.

I remember the guy next me on the plane, oily and expensively suited, who had tried to pick me up. The bubble of poisonous, unreasonable hate I had felt simply because he was Italian made me turn on him with so much revulsion that he shrank back with surprise. But even before we landed in Heathrow I knew I was not broken hearted. It was only my pride that was bruised.

I was not in love with Lupo. I had never allowed myself to be.

He was the most handsome man I knew, other than my brother, Shane, of course. He said all the right things. But he had always revealed his true self in bed. Especially at the beginning of our sexual relationship, when we had sex he would shout out *puttana* as he came. Prostitute. Even after I had asked him not to, he would sometimes slip up. And when I got mad, he apologized and told me it didn't mean anything. It was the same as someone else screaming "Oh God!" during their orgasm. Nevertheless it had never sat well with me. And how right I had been.

After I got back to my mother's house everyone wanted to know why I had left Milan so suddenly.

'Did anyone upset you?'

'Are you ill?'

'Do you no longer want to be an interior designer?'

I never told anyone, especially my second brother, Dominic. Knowing him, he would have taken the first flight out to Milan, beat the shit out of Lupo, and calmly taken the next plane back as if nothing untoward had happened. As far as everyone was concerned, except Maddy, of course, I had come back because I was terribly, terribly homesick.

Now I am determined to start anew in London. On my own. Without any help from my family. I'll get a job like everyone else. Jake told me I could have a try at cutting it on my own, but I had to live in one of his properties. So I moved into one of his London apartments. I was happy because I was only five tube stops away from the apartment Madison shared with her boyfriend.

Absently, I pick up a tub of Greek yogurt from the shelf and place it into my basket. Turning away, I bump into Ria.

She screams with delight. She is wearing a grey blouse, brown leather jacket, faded blue jeans, and purple and orange sneakers. I don't think I have ever seen her look so casual.

'Hi,' I greet and laugh at her infectious joy at bumping into me.

'Just the person I wanted to see,' she exclaims with a huge grin. 'I was going to call you to invite you to come to my birthday party on Saturday. I know it's a bit last minute and all, but it is a last minute plan.'

I smile. 'Twenty-four, right?'

'Yeah, but after this year I'm freezing my age. I'm gonna be twenty-four now until I am fifty, then I will commence the count again.' She laughs her machine gun laugh.

I laugh with her.

'Will you come then?'

'What kind of party is it?' With Ria you have to ask. She's totally unpredictable.

'Dancing and drinking. Nothing big. Just some of my closest friends and family.'

Ria's idea of big is not mine. 'How many people is that?'

'About a hundred,' she says airily.

'You have a hundred close friends?'

'Don't you?' she asks curiously.

I struggle to keep a straight face. 'No, Ria. I don't.'

'Oh!'

'So, where're you having it then?'

'Laissez-faire.'

A warning tinge swirls up my spine. 'Isn't that one of BJ's clubs?'

'Yup. Free drinks all night! Until last week I was going to keep it family only and have a party at my mum's house, but then BJ offered his club and I couldn't believe it.'

'Look Ria. I didn't realize that your birthday was going to be held in London. I am spending the weekend at my Ma's.'

Ria waves my objection aside. 'No problem. BJ has already agreed to pay for cabs for all my single girlfriends.'

I feel trapped. I can't very well tell her I can't go now after I have already agreed. 'Um ... will BJ be there?'

'Well, he promised to drop in, but he said he won't be able to stay for long.'

I breathe a sigh of relief. 'What time?'

'People are going to start arriving around nine but the party will really only get going about ten.'

'OK.'

'When you get to the club just tell them you are there for Ria's party. Oh! And for ID you have to wear red shoes or a red hat.'

'Got it.'

'So what're you up today then?' she asks with a smile.

I shrug. 'Not much. Unsuccessfully looking for a job.'

She frowns. 'Why? Can't one of your brothers give you one?'

'They can but I want to make it on my own.'

'What for?'

'Just to try.'

She looks at me as if I am stupid so I quickly change the subject. 'And where are you off to dressed like that?'

'I'm off to a watch a bit of bare-knuckle fighting.'

'Who's fighting?' I ask, even though it's not too hard to guess.

'I'm putting a hundred quid on BJ,' she says with a cheeky grin.

'What are the odds of him winning?'

"BJ's never lost so the money will be shit. I'm just gonna bet on the amount of punches he has to throw or the minutes the other guy will last. That sort of thing.'

'Sounds exciting,' I say carefully, even though an underground fight where the opponents go on battering each other until one of them can't take it anymore is not my idea of fun. 'And where is it being held?'

'Some godforsaken barn in the sticks. Patrick's taking me. You remember Patrick, my second cousin, don't you?'

'Yes, vaguely,' I say politely. Then words I never intended appear on my tongue. 'Can I come?'

She looks at me sideways. 'Will your brothers be all right with it?'

I know Jake won't be okay with it. Lily told me how he wouldn't even let her watch him fight BJ. But after my humiliating experience in Italy, I've decided that it's time for me to grow up and experience things for myself. Take a few knocks if necessary. I don't want to be the sheltered baby of the family for the rest of my life. I want to see what a bare-knuckle fight looks like. Besides, I'll be with Ria. What can possibly happen to me?

'I won't tell them if you won't,' I tell her.

She giggles conspiratorially. 'My lips are sealed.'

'When are you going?'

'Now.'

I look at my shopping basket. A carton of milk and a pot of Greek yogurt. I take the basket to the check-out counter and give it to the cashier. 'I've changed my mind. Could you please ask someone to put them back on the shelves?'

'Ready?' Ria asks.

'Yeah. I'm ready.'

At that time I am just glad for a new experience. It has not yet occurred to me to do any mischief.

 62

TEN

Layla

In the middle of someone's farm we find a barn that is alive with music and people. We pay our entrance fee and enter. Inside, I gaze around in surprise. The barn is packed to the rafters with far more people than there are cars outside. At a guess, I would say there are at least 300 people. Mostly men, but women of all ages too. Ria tugs my hand.

'Let's place our bets then get a drink. I want to be up front.'

I nod and follow her as she pushes her way through the crowd.

A man in a green sweatshirt and two missing teeth grins at her. 'What'll you have, love?'

'How much will I get if I put a hundred for BJ 'The Bat" Pilkington to win in less than 2 minutes?'

'A hundred and one pounds.'

'One pound profit? For a hundred quid? That's nothing!'

He shrugs. 'The Bat has won 92 fights and drawn once. You're talking about a favorite, a machine that renders men unconscious, love.'

Ria rubs the back of her neck. 'How much for him winning in less than one minute?'

'Twenty.'

'That's just crap. Less than thirty seconds?'

'I'll give you fifty for that.'

She looks at him doubtfully, and then makes her decision. 'All right, I'll just take less than a minute.'

She gives him five twenty pound notes and he passes it to another young man standing behind him, and writes something in his tatty notebook.

He turns to me. 'What about you, young lady?'

'Me? I'm not...' I pause. Why shouldn't I? Why shouldn't I bet like Ria? It's just for fun. 'What would give me a really good payout?'

He grins. 'The Bat to lose.'

'Other than that?'

'That The Devil's Hammer lands a swing on The Bat's face.'

I frown. 'Why's that?'

'Because except for his fight with Jake Eden, The Bat has never been hit in the face.'

'How much will I get for my hundred?'

'Two grand.'

'Wow! That's huge.'

'Yeah, right. The payout's so damn good, because it's never gonna happen. Don't do it, Layla. You might as well burn your money,' Ria advises with a frown.

'I like to live dangerously,' I say with a grin and hold out my money. The bookie secretes it away in single hand movement. Like oil pouring from a drum. A smooth, effortless miracle of nature.

He jots my bet down in his little book and we move away towards the bar. The bar is a collection of huge metal drums filled with beer bottles, ice, and water. We each order a bottle of beer, drinking straight from the bottle since there are no glasses available. I am strangely excited. The mood of the crowd has affected me. There is anticipation in the air.

We go right to the front of the pit, a small area cordoned off with bales of hay, and find ourselves a spot where we have a good view of the fight. In minutes the first fight starts. Two young men, who seem evenly matched to me, start walking towards the pit. One of them takes a step into the pit and establishes his jab straight away. Moving his head from side to side and jogging around. Suddenly, without warning, his clenched fist shoots out. Bang, a body shot that leaves his opponent reeling backwards into the hay. The fight is over in seconds as the aggressor then lunges forwards and knocks him out in one punch.

'Wow,' I say to Ria. 'He's brutal.'

'Wait 'til you see BJ.'

The next fight lasts a lot longer and is astonishingly violent.

I see it then for what it truly is, a festival of physical abuse. Men going for it, egged on by a baying crowd. There is no holding back. It's in their blood. To decide who is the hardest of them all. The sport of legend, guts, honor, and heart.

Both men are bloodied and in bad shape when one of them spits out his mouth guard and falls to his knees. His friends have to carry him away. My heart is pounding hard. That had been too brutal. I hadn't enjoyed it, but all around me the crowd has woken up. A thrill runs through them. An air expectancy hovers over us like that crackle in the air before a thunderstorm.

'BJ is next,' Ria says.

'Now for the fight you have all been waiting for,' the MC announces excitedly. 'Tony "The Devil's Hammer" Radley versus Billy Joe "The Bat" Pilkington.'

The crowd cheers and whistles.

'Tony "The Devil's Hammer" Radley,' the announcer screams over the whistles and calls. Queen's *We Are the Champions* fills the air and BJ's opponent, a huge, bearded man appears. He lifts his hands high over his head in acknowledgement and runs energetically towards the pit.

'And now for the undefeated champion, Billy Joe "The Bat" Pilkington.'

Meatloaf's *Bat Out of Hell* blares out and BJ walks out to the pit. The crowd goes absolutely crazy, clapping and cheering, banging their bottles on the wooden surfaces in the barn. There is no doubting the crowd's favorite.

He is wearing a plain black t-shirt and khaki trousers. As he walks into the pit, I notice that everything about him is different. His eyebrows are drawn straight, his eyes are pitiless, chips of black ice, and his face is devoid of any expression. It is like looking at a cold-blooded psychopath or a heartless machine. I try to imagine this cold, cold monster fighting warm, kind-hearted Jake and feel a tight knot of fear inside. No wonder Jake didn't want Lily to see the fight. This man is exactly what the bookie called him – a machine that renders men unconscious. He is here for one reason and one reason alone: to completely decimate the other man.

He is so different than the BJ I know, I am actually shocked.

The way he angles his head forward combined with his shoulders rounded and his hands slightly curled at the elbows reminds me of a charging bull. At that moment he is the most coldly aggressive man I have seen in my life. He doesn't look at the crowd. He has eyes only for his opponent. My gaze skitters over to The Devil's Hammer. He is holding his hands up in readiness and jabbing the air while jumping around with quick nimble steps, but in his eyes, I see fear. In his head he has already lost. The only question left is how badly he's going to lose.

BJ steps into the pit and ... and like a bull rushes towards him. It is an ambush, clear and simple. Blows rain on the unprepared man's body so quickly and so relentlessly he is overwhelmed by the ferocity of the attack. The Devil's Hammer flails uselessly. One power punch catches him flush on the chin and he flies backwards, landing on one of the hay bales. The crowds bays its approval. But The Devil's Hammer is not beat. There is life in him yet. He pulls himself up painfully, and lunges unsteadily towards BJ.

BJ stands still. Like a bull readying itself for a matador. He doesn't move a muscle. And suddenly I know what he is going to do. It's the oddest thing, but I do. He is going to land the punch that puts The Devil's Hammer to sleep. At the exact moment, as The Devil's Hammer prepares to throw his own punch, I open my mouth, and with all the power in my lungs, scream BJ's name.

'BILLY JOE PILKINGTON.'

Every person in the barn turns startled eyes in my direction. But my eyes are on BJ. He has turned towards my voice, an expression of total incomprehension on his face. I am the last person in the world he expects to see. His eyes find me and he looks as if he has seen a ghost. The Devil's Hammer's punch lands. It socks him in the face. A direct hit. The momentum causes BJ to stagger back slightly. His eyes rush away from me. When he straightens, he is an avenging angel.

He is so furious he looks as if he wants to tear the other man's head off. BJ pummels his opponent with such barbaric brutality that I have to close my eyes. I hear the dull thud of the man falling, then the crowd going crazy. I feel hot and claustrophobic. My heart is beating too fast. I turn towards Ria.

She looks at me strangely. 'Congratulations,' she says. 'You won your bet.'

I nod. People are giving me sidelong glances. I've made a spectacle of myself, but I don't feel embarrassed. In fact, I feel oddly detached. I think I am shocked at myself. At the harm I have caused to another. I have never harmed another human being before. I even hate it when I accidentally snap an insect or a frog in the garden with my hoe.

'Can I borrow a cigarette?' I ask Ria.

'Sure.' She gives me a packet. 'The lighter is inside,' she says.

'Thanks,' I say with a tense smile, and pushing my way out of the barn, go outside. It is freezing. I don't normally smoke, but I feel jittery. Even my hands are shaking. I walk to the side of the barn and light a cigarette. I have taken only one puff when I feel the air around me change. Become thicker. I turn my head slowly. Our eyes touch.

'Are we quits now?' BJ asks.

His left cheekbone is badly swollen and starting to discolor. I turn away from his cold, cold eyes. I feel raw. 'Yeah, we're quits.'

'Can I have one?'

I fit my cigarette between my lips and hold open the cigarette packet. He takes one. There is blood on his hand.

'Does it hurt?' I ask.

'No.'

'Why not?'

'I'm buzzing.'

I flick open the lighter and hold the flame up to him. My hand is shaking. His other hand comes up to cup the flame. In the intimate glow, I see the heat rise from his skin like steam. And I smell the sweat and the trace of endorphins and adrenaline radiating from it. Our eyes meet again and we stare at each other. Yes, I am shocked, and yes, I am shaken, but there is something else struggling to show its face. He inhales, the cigarette burns orange, and I kill the flame with a click.

I turn away, dropping the lighter back into the packet. I return my forefinger and middle finger back on either side of my cigarette and inhale a lungful of warm smoke. It makes me feel light-headed. I exhale it out slowly and put my hand down to the side of my body. There is a foot between us, and an unmistakable element of danger. Like being on one of those roller coasters that inverts you. You are scared to death and unbelievably excited at the same time.

I grasp that I'm not only aroused by the violence I witnessed in the pit, I am excited by the tightly packed, rippling muscles of his body. He is giving off vibes that are calling to me. My life-long hatred of him seems to belong to another place and time. By a strange trick of the light it has morphed into an intense desire to meld my body with his. Shocked by that realization and super aware of him, I carry on staring out into the empty frozen fields.

He doesn't say a word and neither do I. There is nothing to say. Words are superfluous in the wake of the thick, sexual tension crackling like electricity between our bodies.

Suddenly Ria is calling me. 'There you are. I've been looking for you.'

I let the butt of my cigarette drop to the ground and grind it with my foot. I hand her the packet. 'Thanks.'

BJ flicks the end of his cigarette away from him.

'Hey Ria,' he says quietly.

'That was a great fight,' Ria says.

'Thanks,' he says devoid of any emotion. As if he is totally unaffected by her compliment.

My phone rings. I take it out of my purse. Shit. It is my mother. I consider not taking the call, but I know what she's like. She will persist and persist until she gets me.

'Hi Ma.' My eyes flick over to BJ. He is watching me intently.

'Where are you?' she asks.

I gaze down at the frozen ground. 'I'm with Ria,' I reply. I don't dare tell her where I am. I know she won't approve. She'll probably tell Jake and he'll go mad.

'Right. Can you be home in an hour?'

'I guess so. Why?'

'Shane's coming around to your place. I've sent some food for you.'

'Oh, OK.'

'Call me when you get home, OK?'

'Will do.'

'But call Shane first,' she says, and rings off.

I put my phone back into my purse and look up at Ria imploringly. 'I'm sorry, but I've got to get home. My ma is sending my brother around to my place in an hour.'

'Blimey,' Ria says, widening her eyes. 'You better call him and make it an hour and a half.' She turns towards BJ. 'I'll see you this weekend then.'

He nods and looks at me.

'Bye,' I say awkwardly.

Then we are hurrying back into the barn in search of the guy we placed our bets with.

ELEVEN

Layla

Saturday. It takes forever to come, but when it does it brings a hard, tight knot into my stomach.

I know Ria and all her mates will dress to kill, so I take a long time getting ready. I soak in the bath for almost an hour with my mother's secret homemade masque recipe on my face and another of her concoctions in my hair. She claims it's guaranteed to make my hair shine. My mother's potions do a good job, my skin is glowing and my hair glossy and shiny.

I wear my white mini dress. It is sleeveless with a high Nehru collar, but what makes it daring without being slutty is a five-inch long oval cutout in the middle of the dress that reveals my nicely tanned torso and belly button. I stick a red beret on my head and slide into a pair of knee length, white suede peep-toe boots that were all the rage a few months ago in Italy.

I stand in front of the mirror and I know I look good. My thoughts go to that moment when BJ bent his head to me and we shared a flame. Unconsciously, my finger slowly circles my bare belly.

Laissez-faire is a cavernous, totally modern nightclub with under-flooring lights that flash blue and white and gleaming metal structures on the walls and pillars. Ria is having her party in the VIP area upstairs. As soon as I enter the cordoned off area, she runs towards me.

'Oh! My! God!' she screams. 'You look awesome, babe. I LOVE your boots.'

She looks glamorous in a red cowboy hat with a rhinestone band, a tight red and black striped dress, and the highest boots I have seen outside of a fashion magazine.

The lights pick up the glitter on her lovely brown skin.

'Well, you look absolutely stunning yourself,' I tell her sincerely.

She flicks her long, summer-streaked hair. 'You bet I do.'

I smile. None of that false modesty for Ria. I hold out her present, a pretty chain belt I bought in Milan. 'Happy Birthday, Ria.'

She takes it, beaming. 'Thanks. Come on. Let's get you a drink.' She winks at me. 'We're drinking champagne. BJ said we could have anything we wanted, so we ordered bubbly, but we didn't go overboard and get the really expensive stuff though,' she tells me chattily as we cross the room for the bar.

We are halfway there when Ria's favorite song, Justin Timberlake's *Sexy Back,* comes on. With a shout of pure joy she puts her present on the floor, and gyrates provocatively around me. With a laugh I give in. We start bumping hips, twerking comically, and dancing around my present like two demented teenagers. Soon her other friends come onto the floor to join us.

When the song is over, Ria takes my hand and we attempt to continue our journey to the bar, but *All About That Bass* comes on and I love that song. I swing her around and we are at it again.

Laughing and breathless, we reach the bar five songs later. No sooner have we had a sip of our champagne than another of my favorite tracks comes on. Five of us girls rush off to the dance floor and give it all we've got.

The hours pass fast. The music is good and Ria is a great laugh.

It's almost midnight. I know because the girl next to me is whispering that there is a surprise cake to be cut at the exact stroke of twelve. I am sitting at the table with Ria, feeling relaxed and merry when the air shifts. I look up and BJ is standing over us, looming even bigger and broader than I remember. He is wearing a khaki t-shirt tight enough to show off his impressive muscles and the V of his torso. His jeans hang low on his hips.

But he is with a woman!

It takes a few seconds for that to sink in. But when it does—fucking hell!—I feel like the biggest fool this side of the equator. There was nothing between us after all. It was all in my imagination. I was wrong again. Just as I was wrong about Lupo. Without looking directly into his eyes, my eyes slide away to her.

She is voluptuous and hauntingly exotic with creamy skin, blue-black hair, either green or hazel eyes (it's impossible to tell under the club's lights), and high cheekbones that give her a feline appearance. She is wearing a short black dress that can barely contain her curves, and she has her hand possessively curved around BJ's arm. Her nails are long and red and she is running them lightly along the inside of his forearm in a way that is profoundly sexual. I find the sight so disturbing I have to drop my head and stare into my drink.

'Layla,' BJ says by way of greeting.

'Hi,' I reply brightly, looking up, but not letting my eyes rise past his mouth. He has a sexy mouth. The lower lip is so deliciously plump it makes you want to nibble it. Jeez. How much champagne have I had? I return my eyes to my drink. Five glasses.

To my horror Ria invites BJ to sit with us. She slides closer to me, and motions for me to scoot up further along the seat. The space she's freeing up does not seem big enough for him. Fortunately, he tells us that he's not staying. I look up with relief.

Big mistake.

He is staring at me and I am suddenly caught in his stare, unable to look away. I suck my bottom lip into my mouth. There is a curse word stuck behind my teeth. My skin comes alive and my heart dances in my chest.

'Layla. Isn't that an Arabic name that means the dark of the night?' the woman he is with asks with a fake-ass smile.

Before I can answer BJ speaks up. 'No, the real Arabic translation of Layla means

78

that light, giddy feeling one has after the first drink of the night. Not drunk but on the way to being there. It is the beginning of intoxication.'

My breath catches in my throat. I stare at him shocked. The way he said Layla had been a sultry caress.

The woman laughs, a hostile, angry sound. 'Well, Arabic names on non-Arabs is a bit silly, really.'

'I can't imagine a more suitable name for her,' BJ says, his coal black eyes never leaving mine.

Flustered by the look in his eyes, I stand up in a rush. His gaze drops to my navel. His lust is so blatant, fiery heat rushes up my neck and into my face.

'Excuse me. I need to nip over to the ladies,' I tell the girls as I slide out of the banquette seat.

I feel his eyes burning into my back as I leave the sectioned-off area.

I stand in front of the mirror and stare at myself. There are two spots of high color on my cheeks, my hair is an untidy mess, and my beret is no longer set at its jaunty angle. Someone has stepped on the side of one of my beautiful new boots and there is a brown mark on it. I pull out some paper towels from the dispenser, wet them, and try to clean it off, but I have to give up without much success.

The weird thing is, I am doing all these things on autopilot. Some part of my brain

is going crazy. *He came with another woman.* It rankles. But then he goes on about my name and *looks* at me as if he wants to eat me. What's he playing at? Is there or isn't there something between us

I run my fingers through my hair, apply a new layer of lip gloss and exit the toilets. As I walk along the frosted glass corridor a large hand reaches out from the darkness and slams me against an unyielding body.

TWELVE

Layla

What if we kiss? What then?

My breasts are crushed against his hard muscles, but I don't attempt to struggle. I have grown up with three brothers so I know how useless it is to fight with people who are bigger and stronger than you are. Instead I fix him with a venom-filled glare. *He brought a fucking woman with him.*

'Let go of me.'

'Scared?' he taunts, his voice rich and smooth.

'Of you?' I scoff sarcastically, as if even the idea is incredible.

He laughs. It comes from somewhere deep inside him, a wicked rumble. But I like it. I like it a lot.

'Yeah me,' he says. 'I like to tie girls up and suck their pussies until they scream.'

I feel my belly contract. How different this laughing man is from the one who shared a flame with me outside the barn. 'Oh, you are disgusting.'

He holds me at arm's length and lets his eyes travel down, deliberately lingering on my breasts before coming to a stop at my bare belly.

'Will you freaking stop staring at me like that?'

He grins and a dimple pops up in his chin. It makes him look edible. 'If you don't want men to look at you like that, why do you dress like that?'

'You're an asshole, you know?' I huff.

'And you're seriously fuckin' hot.'

My eyes widen. 'Are you fucking serious?' I gasp.

'My balls are already aching.'

'I don't believe this.'

'What sounds do you make when you come?'

'What?' I sputter. This is too much. It's outrageous. He's flirting with me and he has

a woman waiting for him upstairs. What an arrogant bastard. 'How dare you?'

He smiles slowly. The slowest smile I've seen in my entire life. 'If you don't tell me, I'm gonna assume you want me to find out for myself.'

My palm swings upwards furiously, but his hand shoots out and catches it. Bending my fingers inwards he lifts my knuckles up to his lips. I try to jerk my wrist away, but it doesn't move at all. My breathing is erratic and my lips are trembling.

He smiles down at me, his eyes black and frighteningly unknowable.

'You want to expend some energy, wildcat? Give me your address and I'll come around later.'

My chest puffs out. My blood is pounding with fury and lust. I feel as if I am about to explode in his face. I don't know why this man can get me in this state with just the lift of an eyebrow. I shake my head. 'I can't decide if you are thick or just plain stupid. Read my lips. I. Don't. Want. You.'

'My, my, what a little liar you are. That's not at all what your delectable body is telling mine.' He runs a callused finger along the bare skin of my arm. It is not a particularly intimate or sexy move, but the way he does it makes me shiver. I freeze and hold my breath. When he reaches my wrist, he catches it and brings it up to his nose.

'You've never changed your perfume, have you?' His voice is quiet, reflective, but there are black fires burning in his eyes.

My breath comes out in a whoosh. He noticed! I don't tell him that this perfume was the last gift from my father. I had come back from a day of horse riding and my father had given me the box and said, 'A flower shouldn't smell like a donkey.'

'It suits you,' he says, looking at me as if he is drinking me in. I stare up at him stupidly. I am very tall but even in my high-heeled boots he still makes me feel tiny.

The music changes. Chris Isaak's sex anthem, *Wicked Game*, comes on.

'They're playing our song, Layla,' he says in a smoky drawl.

'We don't have a song,' I tell him, but my voice is weak

His eyes gleam with amusement. He bends his head and I jerk back. 'Who told you that?' he whispers, so close to my ear I feel his breath hot and smelling of mints.

Deftly, he whirls me around twice so I am suddenly thrust onto the edge of the dance floor. Isaak's yearning vocals fill the air and I feel something melt inside me. The pulsating bodies around us melt away and we are inside the sexy black-and-white Herb Ritts video. A dreamy place where everything happens in slow motion and I am frolicking with the most gorgeous man on earth.

When Isaak's voice slithers, *'What a wicked game you played to make me feel this way.'* I feel as if BJ is singing it to me. His arms envelop my body tightly, we fit together perfectly. We stare into each other's eyes. Lost in the dream world he has created, I lace my fingers around the back of BJ's powerful neck. The thick muscles contract under my hands. My fingers sweep and tangle in his hair.

'I'd never dreamed I'd love somebody like you'.

I rest my cheek on his chest and listen to the swaggering, strut-worthy tempo of his heart. Everything about him is so macho. Even his heartbeat has attitude. I close my eyes. His intentions are delicious and unapologetically impolite. I don't want to admit it, but some part of me aches for him.

'No IIIIIII don't want to fall in love... with you.'

He lifts me by my waist. I don't scream or yelp. My brothers have been doing it to me for years. When my throat is at his mouth level, he kisses it and I throw my head back and shudder at the warmth. He carries me higher still. I place my palms on his massive shoulders and look down on him. He stares at me, his eyes black and voracious. Slowly he twirls me. Round and round. Our eyes lock on each other. Then he moves his head forward and licks my belly button, like an animal. The carnality of the gesture makes me gasp.

Around us the music begins to slow down.

Isaak says, *'Nobody loves no one.'*

'I've tasted you and you are a meal I wish to devour,' he growls in my ear on my journey back to the ground. My feet touch the ground and my knees feel shaky. This is not a dance. This is a seduction, a kind I have never experienced. Primitive, raw, irresistible.

Dazed with hypnotic lust and mesmerized by his eyes, I gaze wordlessly up into his harsh face. A seduction is a promise of pleasure and release. I'm waiting. I guess I'm waiting for him to deliver. His head swoops down and his mouth captures mine. He kisses like a bandit. A time thieving bandit. Time slips away from me. The kiss goes on and on. I never want it to end. How long I stand within the circle of his arms while his mouth plunders mine I don't know.

Heat and fire flood my belly.

My entire body is a river of sensations. Nothing in my life has ever felt so good. With his hand on the small of my back he presses me even closer into his body as if he wants to meld me into him. As if he wants to completely crush and dominate me.

It is as if there is something inside both of us that is fighting to get to the other. My hips thrust into his thick hardness and I lust for him. The craving for him is like a

 86

fever. When he raises his head, I am such a mess I can do no more than blink stupidly.

Fall Out Boy's *Centuries* comes on around us and Patrick Stump is screaming, *'Remember me ... for centuries.'*

He lets go of me, his eyes narrowed. As ever, a sense of danger, something taboo, lingers around him. 'Meet me tomorrow,' he says. There is a thread of urgency in his voice.

The burn of his kiss lingers, and his scent is clinging to my skin like a touch. Nobody has ever kissed me like that. 'I can't. I'm going back to London tomorrow night.'

'Come for dinner on Monday.'

'Dinner,' I repeat stupidly.

'At Pigeon's Pie.'

Pigeon's Pie is one of his pubs. I hesitate.

'You can bring Ria with you,' he urges persuasively.

I shake my head and start backing away from him. 'No,' I whisper. I don't want to be another girl he's fucked and kicked to the curb. It would kill me.

'I'll be waiting for you,' he says.

I turn around and run into the crowd of people.

Up on his high station the DJ yells, 'Show some fucking mercy. Put your hands up,' and starts playing my most favorite song in the whole wide world. *Are you with me?*

BJ

I watch her run away in those crazy boots, boots that make me want to suck her cute little princess toes. I bet they smell like flowers. 'You can run little Sapphire Eyes, but you can't hide.'

This is the most exposed, terrified, and exhilarated I've ever been. It feels as if all the blood has drained from my head and gone into my cock. Across the crowd I spot my manager and walk over to him.

'Hey BJ,' he greets politely.

I nod curtly. He's good at his job, but I keep the demarcation clear at all times. We're not friends. He works for me. I'm his boss. This way nobody oversteps the mark.

'There's a girl with a red beret, white suede boots, and a white dress who is here for Ria's party. Find her and watch her like a hawk. Anyone that tries to chat her up, throw them out.'

His eyes bulge. He has never received an instruction like that from me before.

'Got that?' I ask, a little more aggressively than I had intended.

'Yeah, yeah, I got that,' he replies quickly, his hands coming up defensively.

'Good. Did you see the woman I came in with?'

'Yeah,' he admits warily.

'Call her a taxi when she's ready to go home.'

'Okay,' he says, with a smile of relief.

'Any problems with red beret call me on my mobile regardless of the time.'

'Got it.'

'Good. Have a good night.'

'Goodnight and thank you, BJ.'

I turn around. 'Oh, one other thing, make sure you escort red beret to her taxi.'

THIRTEEN

Layla

By the time I wake up light is filtering in all around the edges of the curtains. I peer at my bedside clock and see with surprise that it is almost eleven. I must have been more tired than I realized. Strange my mother didn't come to wake me up. I'd told her I wanted to help prepare Sunday lunch. I stretch luxuriously in the dim coolness of my childhood bed. And then the memory comes rushing back and my hand reaches for my mouth.

He kissed me!

A smile creeps onto my lips. I sit up and grab the teddy bear sitting on the shelf over my bed. I slide back under the warmth of the duvet, hugging my bear tightly. His name is Graystone and he is nearly 20 years old, but he has been well cared for and looks exceptional for his age. He smells of lavender. Once a month my mother opens his neck and stuffs him with sachets of dried lavender flowers. When I was very young, I used to have conversations with my bear and I honestly believed he would reply.

'Don't tell anyone, Graystone,' I whisper into his sweet-smelling head. 'But it was mind-blowingly hot, like nothing I have ever experienced. It almost made me dizzy.'

Graystone stays silent.

I sigh softly. 'I know. I know. He made it abundantly clear that it's just sex he's after, but so what?'

Last night I was a bit tipsy and had persuaded myself that I didn't want to be just another notch on his bedpost, but in the cold light of day, why not? This is the new, adventurous me. Besides there's always been this thing between us. Why not give in and just let it burn itself out. I'm not in any danger. It's just a physical thing. I *know* I won't fall in love with him or anything crazy like that. I mean I don't really even like the man.

I replay the dance, the kiss, the extraordinary way he had licked me as if he was claiming his territory. I touch my belly button and feel an immediate reaction between my legs. Wetness! It was never like this with Lupo or anyone before him.

I put Graystone back on the shelf and roll out of bed, determined not think of BJ until tomorrow when I'll decide whether or not to turn up at Pigeon's Pie. I open my bedroom door and hear the sounds of my brothers' voices downstairs. Still in my pajamas and without going to the bathroom first or making myself look presentable, I run down the stairs and into the living room. My mother is sitting in her armchair and my three brothers are sitting on the long sofa talking to her.

They all turn towards me.

'Sleeping Beauty is awake,' Shane says.

'Hello, sleepyhead,' Jake greets. I go over to the sofa and standing at the armrest, let myself fall like a felled tree into my brothers' laps. Just like I have been doing since I was a child.

'Timber,' Dominic calls and they catch me, laughing.

'Layla, you're not a little girl anymore. You're far too old to be doing such unladylike things,' my mother disapproves.

'No, she's not,' Shane rushes to my defense.

'Stop spoiling her,' my mother scolds him, but her voice lacks any real conviction.

Secretly, she is proud of how close her family is. 'She's old enough to be a mother herself,' she adds grumpily.

'Perish the thought. She's still just a baby herself,' Jake says lazily, gently sweeping hair out of my face.

'She's never going to be too old for this even when she is 90,' adds Dominic, who is sitting in the middle. With a growl he begins to tickle my belly. Suddenly all of them have gotten into the act and there are hands everywhere, in my armpits, my ribs, my belly. With a yelp I try to wriggle and evade their roaming hands, but their grip is steel-like and there are too many hands coming from all sides. Helpless, I laugh until I am gasping for air and my stomach hurts.

'I haven't been to the toilet yet. I'm gonna wee on you,' I splutter desperately.

It works instantly. They stop immediately and I worm off them and land on the floor on my back, breathless and panting.

My brothers look down at me indulgently, but my mother is tutting away. I turn my head towards my mother's upside down face.

'I thought you were going to wake me up and let me help you with lunch.'

'I heard you stumbling around at two in the morning. I wanted you to have a good rest. You look better for it. Anyway, everything is done. Go and make yourself presentable. Lunch is in an hour.'

'Thanks, Ma.' I grin at her, then I turn my head back towards Jake. 'Where is Lily?'

'She was feeling a bit tired. She's lying down in Ma's room.'

I frown. I really like Lily. There is something so delicate and sweet about her. 'She's okay, right?'

'Yeah, she's fine.'

I sit up. 'OK, I'm going to go say hello. See you guys after I have peed.'

I run up the stairs towards my mother's room. Outside her door I knock softly and call, 'Lily?'

'Come in,' she says instantly.

I open the door and she is trying to sit up. She is already eight months pregnant and her belly is quite big for her tiny frame.

'Don't sit up,' I tell her and she lies back down.

I go up to her. 'Can I listen?'

She smiles.

I crouch next to the bed, put my ear against her stomach, and listen to my niece. For a few seconds everything is quiet. Then I distinctively hear a noise.

'What can you hear?' Lily asks.

'I think she just hiccupped,' I tell her.

Lily laughs. 'You're as bad as your brother. He swears he can hear her laugh.'

I look at her incredulously. 'Really?'

She looks at me and shakes her head. 'Through amniotic fluid? Very doubtful. But, to be fair, when he puts his head on my stomach she will shift around excitedly and kick hard. As if she recognizes her father.'

I look at her in wonder. 'Wow, how amazing is that?'

She chuckles softly. 'It is when you think about it.'

I sit cross-legged on the floor with an elbow resting at the edge of my right knee and my chin in my palm. 'Tell me about the day when you found out you were pregnant. I want to know everything. How you told Jake. And then what he said and did.'

She smiles with the memory. 'Well, I guess I knew I was pregnant two days after I missed my period. I'm like clockwork. So I bought a couple of pregnancy tests and both were positive. The funny thing is, it was one day before the first anniversary of the day we met, so I decided not to tell him until our anniversary night. We were going to spend it in Paris and I wanted to tell him at the hotel before we went to dinner.'

She looks away from me, a dreamy, far-away look in her eyes.

'He had booked us this beautiful hotel suite in Paris. It had one of those impossibly glamorous interiors, you know, the ones you see in movies. With tall, gilded ceilings, wall paneling, antique wooden floors, and a massive, intricately-carved gold bed. It had a three balconies and palm trees in Chinese pots. That's where I told him.'

She pauses and there are tears in her eyes.

'Oh Lily, you are crying.'

She shakes his head. 'It was just so beautiful. I had bought these little yellow shoes. They were the tiniest pair of knitted shoes you ever saw. They came in a white cardboard box and I had asked the girl in the shop to gift-wrap them. I still remember the wrapping. Yellow with red balloons. So just before we left for dinner I put the box into his hand. "For you," I said. He frowned, holding the small box in his hand as if it was the most precious thing in the world. "For me?" he asked as he did not quite believe it. You see, until then I had never given him anything. What could I give him? He was the man who had everything.'

She smiles, a glowing secret smile.

'He opened the box. For a while he simply stared at them incredulously and then he fished them out between his thumb and forefinger and looked at me. Oh Layla, you should have seen the expression on his face. It gives me goosebumps even now. He was so happy, but he didn't dare believe it, just in case it was a stupid joke or it meant something different. "Are you trying to tell me what I think you're trying to tell me?" he whispered.'

'I just nodded and watched as he carefully put the shoes back into the box, and put the box on the side table. Then, with a crazy, small boy whoop of pure joy, he lifted me up into the air and whirled me round and round until I was quite, quite dizzy.'

'Oh Lily,' I breathe. 'What a lovely story.'

'It *was* an unforgettable night,' she says softly, and strokes her belly with a contented sigh.

'I don't know if I'll ever find the kind of love you have.'

She looks me in the eye. 'Sometimes the man for you is closer than you think.'

BJ's face flashes into my mind. How would such an obviously cold and hard man react to the news he is going to be a father?

'One day you'll be pregnant and when you tell your man you're carrying his child you will know exactly what I mean. A light, a special light, comes into his eyes.'

For a while we stop speaking. Each of us lost in our own thoughts. Then Lily breaks the silence. 'Your mum said you went to a party at Laissez-faire last night.'

'Yeah,' I admit. 'It was Ria's birthday party.' I briefly consider telling her about BJ, about that slow-motion, sex-drenched dance and the drug-like kiss afterwards. Then I decide not to. Nothing has happened yet. Nothing will if I don't make it to Pigeon's Pie.

'Was it good?'

I grin. 'It was brilliant. The music was great and we danced all night, but there was a big fight at the end. A guy almost crashed into me, but I was lucky. The manager of the

club appeared out of nowhere and pulled me out of harm's way. He immediately called a taxi and insisted on putting me into it. Very decent of him, I thought.'

Lily's eyes have an oddly knowing glint and she looks as if she is about to say something, but at that moment Jake enters the room, and I run off to the toilet. After I brush my teeth and hair, I dress in a pair of old jeans and a huge, comfy jumper. Then I run downstairs to join my family.

Lunch is fun. It always is when my brothers are around. Jake is the oldest and he took on the role of breadwinner when my father died, making him the lucky one I run to when I am in trouble. Then there's Dominic. He is a hothead with a hair-trigger temper, but he has a soft spot for me, so I can generally get away with murder with him. He's the one I go to when I've done something I shouldn't have and need to be forgiven.

Shane is only a year older than me. He's the coolest of my brothers, I can totally relax with him and say and do anything I want. He is also the most classically handsome Eden brother and the playboy of the family. He's got girls everywhere. When we go out together I get a ton of venomous and jealous looks from women. I almost pity the woman he will end up with. It must be hell to be with such a player.

Shane catches my eye and taps the handle of his knife so it hits the table surface

and expertly flicks a pea in my direction. I open my mouth and in it goes.

'Stop it, both of you.' My mother looks at Shane sternly. 'Layla is *not* a child.'

Both of us erupt into irrepressible laughter.

My mother turns to me. 'By the time I was your age I was married with four children.'

'Shane started it,' I say.

'This is not proper behavior for a lady. Do you want people to think I raised a hooligan?' my mother asks.

I cast my eyes down.

'Let her be, Ma,' Dominic, ever the gallant, comes to my rescue. 'When she was away you were always moaning that it was like the life and soul of this family went away. All our meals were proper and dull. Now she's back and you won't let her have a bit of fun. She doesn't behave like this when we are out. This is our family meal. Let her have her fun.'

I look at Dominic with astonishment. My mum said that.

To my surprise Jake cuts in. 'It's true that we spoil Layla rotten, but she hasn't turned out so bad. She knows right from wrong. She's never ever mean to anyone. She's generous to a fault. She wouldn't hurt a fly. She's not stubborn or selfish or bossy or bitchy. Quite frankly, she makes me proud of her.'

'And she knows how to catch flying peas in her mouth,' Shane adds with a grin.

Everybody laughs. Even my mother smiles.

I gaze around the table at all their faces, even the latest addition, Lily, and my heart brims over with love. At that moment I think I am the most blessed person in the entire world

'How's the job search coming along, Bear?' Jake asks.

'I've got an interview on Wednesday. Fingers crossed,' I say and stuff a chunk of roasted potato into my mouth so that he can't ask where it is. Jake is such a control freak, he actually paid the people living in the flat next to me in Milan to keep an eye on me and make sure I was all right! God knows what he will do if I tell him where my interview is.

'Mmmm ... delicious, Ma,' I say around my food.

My mother makes the best roasted potatoes ever. Her secret is twofold. She strains the potatoes and gives them a good hard shake in a closed lid pot after they have been cooked to break up their edges. Then she drops them on a baking tray of very hot goose fat. Hot enough to make the potatoes sizzle. The result: crispy on the outside, billowy on the inside.

After lunch Jake and Lily offer me a lift back to London, a suggestion I quickly accept.

FOURTEEN

Layla

The journey is pleasant. The conversation is light and easy and it is only when Jake and Lily start talking about attending a wedding of a family friend that I kind of put my foot in it.

'Do you want to go, Bear?' my brother asks.

'Will BJ be there?' I reply.

Jake meets my eyes in the rearview mirror. He is frowning. 'Why do you want to know?'

I shrug. 'Just curious.'

'Stay away from BJ, Layla,' he warns in a steely voice.

I am immediately curious. 'Why? I thought the feud is over and we are best friends with the Pilkingtons now.'

'We're not best friends. We're friends,' he corrects.

'Ma said he saved your life.'

'Yes, he did and I'll be forever grateful for that, but I don't want him anywhere near my sister. He's a junkyard dog. He'll fuck anything in a skirt.'

'Oh, I don't know,' Lily says. 'I think BJ can be tamed. He is a bit of a beast, but a very seductive beast,' she says and flashes a wink in my direction.

The car suddenly stops.

'Out of the car, you,' Jake tells Lily. His voice is deadly quiet.

She raises her eyebrows at him, then flicks her eyes in my direction, as if asking, *You want to do this with you sister here?*

'I'm waiting,' he says.

'Are you serious?' she asks incredulously.

I look from one to the other curiously.

Jake doesn't reply. Instead he gets out of the car. As I watch totally bemused, he comes around to her side, opens Lily's door, and takes her hand to pull her out and lead

her around the back of the car. For a few moments I don't turn around to look but then, oh fuck it, I have to know. I glance back, and my mouth drops open.

Whoa, Jake!

Lily is being crushed in Jake's arms. He is kissing the shit out of her. The domination and forcefulness of his embrace is astonishing. I didn't know he had it in him to be so intensely jealous and possessive. I swivel my head back quickly, not wanting to be caught staring like a half-wit at my brother eating his wife's face by the roadside. I needn't have worried though. It's a good few minutes before he settles Lily back in the passenger seat. Her cheeks are bright red. And no wonder.

He gets into his seat and turns around to face me.

'You've been warned. BJ saved my life. So I owe him big time, but if he hurts even a hair on your head I'll have to break his fucking legs, and I really don't want to do that. We've just made up with the Pilkingtons after centuries of pointless feuding. If you don't want to start an all-out war again between our families, stay away from him. Can you do that?'

I nod slowly.

'Good. He's not the only man in the world. There are millions of good guys out there for you. You don't need to pick a drug dealer.' He pauses. 'He's a criminal, Layla.

Don't ever mistake him for anything else. You deserve better than him. Much better.'

'Ok,' I whisper.

He turns around and starts the car. We drive the rest of the way in complete silence.

'Thanks for the ride, Jake. Bye, Lily,' I say, opening the car door.

'No problem. I'll wait until you get in,' Jake says.

'You don't have to, Jake. What can possibly happen to me in broad daylight?'

'Layla,' he sighs wearily.

'OK, OK,' I say and, slipping out of the car and shutting the door, I run up the steps to my front door. I love my family to death and all, but sometimes they are so overprotective I feel stifled. I close my front door and I hear Jake's car drive away. My flat is quiet and still. So much so I jump when my phone rings. It's Madison.

'Hey, Maddy. How's it going?'

'Same old, same old,' she says, sounding bored. 'How was your party last night?'

I take a deep breath. 'I kissed ... someone.'

'Wait one moment,' she says and I hear her moving around, doing something. 'Right. I'm back.'

'What were you doing?' I ask.

'Getting a tub of ice cream out of the freezer. So ... who, what, where, when? Spit it out,' she demands bossily.

So I tell her.

'No fucking way!' she screams so loudly I have to hold the phone away from my ear.

I open the freezer and take out a carton of chocolate-chip ice cream and open it on the granite countertop.

'Are you kidding me?' she asks incredulously.

'Nope,' I say, getting a spoon out of a drawer and shutting it with my hip.

'But you hate him!'

I sigh, plonking myself on a stool and stabbing my spoon into the ice cream. 'I know.'

'What do you mean you know? Is this like some sort of a hate fuck?'

'I'm not sure I'm taking it any further than dinner.'

'Liar,' she accuses.

I slide the spoon into my mouth and let the ice cream melt on my tongue. Maddy is right. In my heart of hearts I know I'm not walking away.

'So what are you going to wear tomorrow then?' she asks.

'I don't know yet.'

'Wear your red dress.'

'No way. That's a summer dress.'

'You won't be wearing it for long, anyway.'

'Even if I do decide to go further, I'm not planning on sleeping with him tomorrow.'

'Of course, you're not. You're just practically salivating through the phone and into my ear,' she says with her mouth full.

I scoop more ice cream. 'Want to bet I don't sleep with him tomorrow?'

'To be really frank, I'd sleep with him.'

The spoon halts mid-way. 'What?'

'Wouldn't be the saddest day of my life.'

I lick the spoon. 'Really?'

'Yeah, he has badditude and that intense, laser stare going on.'

I grin. Badditude and a laser stare. That's one description for BJ.

'I like the way he fills out his jeans from the back too,' she adds.

I laugh outright.

'Oh! And I suspect he'll be very good in bed. He looks like he gets laid often.'

That observation shouldn't have troubled me, but it does. Which is strange because after Jake's warning I am of the mind that even if I do sleep with him it will only be the once or twice.

'So come on, what are you going to wear?'

'Something subtle. Maybe a white shirt and my dark green trousers.'

'Isn't that what you were planning to wear for your job interview?'

'No, I was going to wear my black trousers to the interview. I just don't want to give the impression that I'm a slut.'

She laughs. 'You? A slut? Pleeeease. You've got 'Don't Touch' written across your forehead.'

'I do not.'

'All right, I'm wrong. You've got Don't Fucking Touch Or I'll Call The Police blazing from your forehead.'

'Don't exaggerate, Maddie.' I sigh. 'Actually, I'm a bit confused.'

'About what?' she demands.

'I think I'm torn between excitement and panic,' I reveal.

'I get the excitement bit, but why the panic?'

'Because I know it's a bad idea.'

'Why?'

'Well to start with, Jake has threatened me off in no uncertain terms. Absolutely don't go there stuff. Forbidden in capital letters. Huge family feud stuff. Jake actually called him a drug dealer and criminal. And he didn't say it just for effect. He really believes BJ is a massive gangster.'

'Ooook. You said to start with. What are the other reasons?'

'I sometimes get the uneasy feeling that I am standing at the edge of a cliff and about to jump in when I'm with BJ. There's this feeling of doing something deliciously destructive, but there is also the prospect of oblivion forever.'

'Man, only you can make a simple fuck sound so dramatic.'

FIFTEEN

Layla

If a girl will walk stark-naked by the light of
the full moon round a field or a house, and
cast behind her at every step a handful of
salt, she will get the lover whom she desires.
Old Gypsy Magic

The moment Ria called to ask if I wanted
to go to dinner with her at Pigeon's Pie I
knew. I was always going to say yes. So I

did. Ria and I agreed to meet at a wine bar in Waterloo first for one drink and then take a taxi to Pigeon's Pie.

I arrive first. Nervously I order a glass of white wine and find us a table. Ria is dressed in a skin-tight leopard print crop top and leather trousers. She looks sexy and carefree. Suddenly I wish I had taken Maddy's advice, and not dressed so stuffily. We drink a glass of wine and chat about the people we know, then Ria looks at her wristwatch.

'We should go. We don't want to be late for dinner,' she says with a smile.

'No, we don't want to be late,' I agree nervously.

The taxi drops us across the road from Pigeon's Pie. From outside it looks like an old fashioned pub; a place with fruit machines, patterned carpets, dark wood furniture, and horrible pub food.

'You okay?' Ria asks.

'Totally,' I reply and follow her through the double doors. Inside it is exactly as I had envisioned. Only it is surprisingly full of elegantly dressed, well-heeled people.

'Come on,' Ria says and leads me to a back room. She opens the door to a wood paneled room, and—oh my God!—It's like I have been transported into an old gangster movie. This is the proverbial backroom where shady deals get struck. It even has another door, presumably a quick, back way escape door. BJ is sitting at a wooden table and there is a half-drunk pint of Guinness in front of him.

BJ

Forswear it sight! For I ne'er saw true beauty till tonight.

-William Shakespeare, Romeo and Juliet

Oh Layla. Look at you. Dressed as if you're going to a job interview at a bank. A pink and white striped shirt, a tailored, almost masculine black jacket, and the unsexiest article of clothing I've ever had the misfortune to come across: a below the knee, wrap around skirt in gunmetal grey.

Still, it's shocking how relieved I am to see her. Some part of my brain can't believe

she came. Of her own free will. I rise to my feet.

'Hey BJ,' Ria calls out with a big, friendly smile.

'Hey Wild Cat,' I reply easily.

She pouts prettily and lifts her face up to kiss me on the cheek. While her lips are stuck to my face, I shift my gaze to Layla. Her teeth are sunk into her bottom lip. Fuck! What a great mouth. And there's another inch in my pants. Ria dislodges herself with a wet sound.

'Layla.' My eyes take a lazy trip down her body. Jesus! I am crazy-lusting after her.

Color creeps up her cheeks, but her voice is cool. 'BJ.'

'Have a seat,' I invite. 'What do you girls want to drink?'

A waitress has already entered the room and is hovering nervously in the background.

'Champagne,' Ria says, perching delicately at the end of the chair opposite me.

I raise an eyebrow at Layla. 'The same?'

She shrugs. 'OK,' she agrees and slips into the chair next to Ria.

'Bring us a Bollinger,' I tell the waitress.

She nods and scurries away as if I bite. I sit down and lean back, curling my hand loosely around my pint glass.

 111

'Do you still have Bertie?' Ria asks.

'Of course. She's a dead woman if she leaves me.'

Layla's eyes open wide.

Ria laughs. 'Yeah right. You're dead if she leaves you, you mean.'

Ria turns to Layla. 'Bertie was a housecleaner in Florida and came here to visit her niece who was going out with BJ. The niece invited BJ to their home, Bertie cooked him a meal, and the rest is history. She's amazing. She takes American comfort food and fuses it with European, Mexican, and Asian recipes. You won't believe how good they come out. Hard to imagine, but all those posh people out there, they could go to the best restaurants in London, instead they come here for Bertie the housecleaner's food.'

'Wow.'

She turns to me. 'But you prefer the plain comfort food though, don't ya?'

'Give me a plate of fried chicken and I'm a happy man,' I say lightly.

Ria laughs. 'I love coming here.'

The champagne arrives, gets poured, and the girls take their polite little sips.

There is the sound of birds tweeting. It has Ria reaching into her purse for her phone. She looks at the screen, frowns, and says, 'Sorry, I have to take this.'

'Of course,' Layla says.

I gaze at her expressionlessly.

'Oh no,' she exclaims dramatically. 'Noooo. Really? Do you want me to come over?'

I turn my attention to Layla. She is staring at Ria worriedly.

'Don't worry. I'll take a cab. I'll be with you in 20 minutes at the most. No, no, of course not. No, they won't mind.'

She ends the call and looks at me then Layla. 'I'm so sorry, but a friend of mine has just gotten some bad news. I've got to go and be with her. I hope you guys don't mind.'

I shake my head.

Layla says nothing. Just stares at Ria.

Ria turns to me. 'You will give Layla a ride back home, won't you?'

'Sure, I'll give Layla a ride,' I say.

SIXTEEN

Layla

One corner of his mouth crooks up. I love his mouth. The way he says ride is slow and sexy. I bet he can give me a ride. Silently, I watch Ria glug her champagne down as fast as is humanly possible. Her eyes drift longingly to the bottle, but she stands and comes towards me. I allow her to hurriedly air peck both my cheeks and watch while she does the same to BJ. Then she is gone.

And I meet his eyes. 'There's no emergency is there?'

Utterly unperturbed he grins. 'Of course not.'

I stand up.

He looks up at me. His eyes are no longer lazy, and tame. They are unblinking and burning with a fire-like intensity. 'You're all grown up now, Layla. You don't really need a chaperone, do you?'

'No, but I don't appreciate being manipulated.'

'Would you have come on your own?'

I pause. 'I guess not.'

'Do you want me to call Ria back?' he asks gently.

My shoulders sag. Of course I don't. I know what I'm here for. My anger is totally irrational, a result of nervous energy.

'Sit down,' he says softly. 'I promise it'll be the best fried chicken you'll ever eat.'

I take a deep breath and reoccupy the chair I'd vacated. He smiles.

There is something about this man .... Even when he was 15 and I had convinced myself that I thoroughly disliked him, he was still that tough insouciant who stared at me. Now that he's all grown up and forbidden to me, his magnetism whispers and beckons irresistibly. I want him. I want him more than I've wanted anything else in my life. I want him so much it's an ache somewhere deep inside me.

'Are you hungry?' he asks casually, the tone totally at odds with what I see in his eyes.

The reptilian brain lurking inside my head is not in the mood for pillow talk or cuddles or food. It wants what it wants. And what it wants is a fuck. A mindless fuck of epic proportions.

I shake my head and stare at his sexy mouth hungrily.

He lifts his eyebrows. 'You're radiating sex right now.'

My breath comes faster. 'Oh yeah?'

His nostrils flare. 'Yeah. You're giving me a raging hard-on.'

God that was delivered deep and sexy. Strange, my family made me believe I was made of sugar and spice and everything nice, and I have turned out to be made of an inner itching that makes me lewd and lusting.

I stand up and walk over to the door to turn the lock.

He stands up. 'Come and show me how wet you are.'

I walk towards him. When I am about three feet away, I leap up on him, loop my arms around his neck, and curl my legs around his hips, making sure to rub my damp panties against the hard bulge in his jeans.

His large hands curl around my thighs. 'Now you're talking, Princess.'

I lick my lower lip slowly.

He groans. 'Holy shit, Layla.'

I lean closer to his ear, my breath hot. 'What about the fried chicken?'

'Fuck the fried chicken.'

I look up at him from under my lashes. 'How about that ride then?'

'Time you were in my bed, young lady,' he growls and carries me with my wet pussy stuck to the fierce erection in his jeans. We go through a second door in the room that leads to a dim, narrow corridor lit only by an emergency light. I clasp my fingers tightly around his neck and feel like a tick hanging on to the neck of a huge beast.

His skin is warm and he smells wild, like the sea when it is stormy or the forest at night. And ale, I get a whiff of that too. I lay my cheek on his chest and hear his heart beating fast and loud under his clothes. The corridor leads to another emergency door that opens out to the cold night.

Snowflakes fall on his cheeks. I reach up and lick one. His skin feels hot. He leans imperceptibly closer. There is naked need in his eyes. I stare up at him and watch as his breath frosts before it reaches my face.

'When I find something I want to keep, I never let go,' he says quietly.

I smile.

He lifts my shirt and puts his fingertips on my belly.

I shudder. 'Cold.' But I don't jerk away. I don't want him to take his hand away.

He stops in front of a massive, souped up four-wheel drive. More lorry than car. He opens the passenger door and deposits me inside as if I weigh no more than a child. He closes the door, gets into the driver's seat, turns on the noisy engine, and we hurtle through the cold streets of London.

'Where are we going?'

He glances at me before returning his eyes to the road. 'Do you really care?'

He's right. I don't. We don't say a word after that. Sometimes I look sideways at him, but he has his head turned towards the traffic and his profile is stern, his jaw clenched tight. When he briefly looks at me his eyes are glittering and as cold as that of a serpent.

I wonder what he is thinking. I don't ask. It feels like this is what we were meant to do. Always. The dislike was a temporary cover for this volcano of passion and lust.

When we reach his house, he turns to me. In the light of the street lamp, his eyebrows are a straight line under which pools of blackness have gathered. The scar on his face seems alive. He is the most intimidating and magnetic man I have ever met.

'Last chance to back out,' he warns. In the strange shadows his entire body seems to be crouched, tense and waiting. The potty-mouthed bastard is gone. I've never seen him look so grim or so apprehensive. At that moment I know that this is one of those times when I hold all the cards. When my decision will change everything forever.

Both of us know this cannot and will never be just a one-night stand. There will be no going back from this. It will be messy. Other people will get involved. And the inevitable break-up will be heartbreaking. My family will be hurt. I blank out the implications even as Jake's face swims into my consciousness. *Make no mistake. He is a criminal.* This is a guy who gets laid a lot. I close my eyes. It can be a secret. It can be our secret. No one else needs to know. When it burns out, only I will suffer.

'No thanks,' I whisper.

His body becomes slack with relief. He got the girl again. He nods. 'Thank God,' he says savagely triumphant. 'My balls are aching like they've been sucker punched. I need to have my cock in your hot little cunt as soon as possible.'

He hauls open the door on my side, scoops me into his arms, and carries me off to his lair. I look up into his face. Who'd have thought?

Him and me.

SEVENTEEN

Layla

He kicks the front door shut behind him. The house is semi-dark and his footsteps echo. He obviously doesn't use this place much. There is a lamp lit in one of the rooms, its light spilling out into the hallway. He takes me up the stairs, opens a door, and lays me down on a very large bed. Silently, he moves to the fireplace and lights it. A gas fire throws up dancing flames and the sparse room becomes full of shadows.

He turns to me, an odd expression on his face, as if he is stunned to find me in his living space. There is almost an animal-like quality about him. Like a wolf that is crouched and tense, ready to spring on its prey. I drink him in, mesmerized by how large he is, how desperately I want him. He hesitates, as if his next move matters, then walks up to me and says, 'Play with yourself until you are wet and hot.'

'I'm already wet and hot,' I gasp.

'I want to see your pussy dripping. I want to be able to smell you from here. Can you do that for me?'

He emits heat like a radiator. I feel his power flow from his skin and envelop me like a mist. I don't know why, but I do not feel the slightest bit shy. I lift my skirt so he will have a clear view and, spreading my legs, slowly slip my hand into my panties and over my mound. I look up at him and deliberately push my finger deep into my slick channel. My sex is so swollen and engorged with lust that a moan oozes out of me. The sound is thick and so full of need that it is a revelation even to me.

He stands very still, a stranger, watching me avidly. As if this is the first time a woman has ever opened her legs for him.

'I'm dripping,' I groan, my legs squirming. I've never been so hot or so wet before.

'Show me.'

The ache is so strong it feels as if I am bruised between my thighs. I slide my panties over my legs and feet.

He catches me by my ankles, pulls my legs apart, and looks down at me. No man has ever looked at me the way he is looking. As if he is looking at the most beautiful thing he has ever seen in his life. Possessively and with pure, unadulterated yearning. It is addictive. I feel as high as I did that time I had a puff of weed behind the bicycle shed with Willow and her boyfriend. The knots in the thick muscles of his shoulders tell me how much control he is exerting over himself.

His gaze travels back to my face and our eyes lock. His are deliberately hooded, the half-moons holding a force that seems unsuitable for a junkyard dog willing to mate with anything in a skirt. It's more like something you would encounter in a slow-moving, achingly beautiful dream. I want him to enter me so bad my entire body feels like one exposed raw nerve.

'Take off your top,' he growls.

I pull it roughly over my head.

'Lose the bra.'

That went the way of the top pretty damn quick.

He grasps me by my waist as if I am a doll of little consequence or weight and turns me on my face. I hear him unzip my skirt and pull it down my legs. He turns me back around.

 122

'I want to see you play with your nipples.'

I rub my fingers in circles and then catch them between my thumb and forefinger and roll them. His eyes widen.

He kneels down and a shock of black hair falls onto his forehead. My body rises off the bed as my hand moves helplessly to it. I claw my hand through his hair. He remains still, silent, powerful. *I like to tie girls up and suck their pussies until they scream.*

'Make me scream,' I whisper.

'Thought you'd never ask,' he says and slips his palms under my buttocks turning my crotch into a sort of plate or bowl and brings me to his mouth. For a second he looks like a beast about to devour me. And that aura of dominance turns me to mush. I cream. Slickness runs down the insides of my thighs. He extends his hot tongue, swipes it along the crack, and swirls the tip over my plumped, engorged folds.

There is not an inch he does not explore, tease, or brush. Down one side, up the other, this way, that way, a poke here, a brush there ... until my pussy is on fire and I am out of my mind with need, squirming and begging for release.

He sucks my clit and the molten heat of his mouth is such a shock to my system it makes my whole body shake. I come so fucking hard I scream. He doesn't take his huge head away from my oversensitive,

pulsating clit and the orgasm goes on and on. The muscle contractions come and come until my head spins. It is raw, primal, and violent, unlike anything I have ever experienced.

'Whoa, that was amazing,' I whisper, in my stupor.

'Good. Because I'm ready to fuck.'

He pulls his t-shirt over his head and I gape. Holy shit! He is covered in tats. My brothers have them, but not like this. I let my eyes rove over them. Angels, demons, patterns, and the words No Fear blazing across his chest. He unbuttons his fly and his trousers hit the floor. He pulls down his underwear and his cock springs out. My eyes widen. Holy shit fuck! That is the biggest, angriest cock I have ever seen in my life. Swollen and decorated with throbbing veins it is literally jerking with aggression and animal vigor.

'So this is what all the fuss is about,' I say wonderingly. Now I know why he wanted me to be dripping wet.

'Don't fret, hun. Just spread your legs a bit wider,' he advises as he rolls a condom over the massive shaft.

Eagerly I splay my legs as far as they will go. He lifts both my wrists over my head and traps them under his large hand. Staring in my eyes he slowly sinks his massive cockhead into me, forcing my pussy to accommodate him. He is so big my mouth opens in a silent cry of shock. I've never been so stretched before or so damn full.

'Fuck, your cunt is incredibly tight,' he rumbles deep in his throat.

Unable to talk, I take a shallow breath, and he uses that opportunity to push himself even deeper into me.

Oh God. Yes.

'You like having a big dick inside you, Princess Layla?'

Vulnerable and totally exposed, I nod.

He pushes again. And he is balls-deep inside.

I expel the breath I was holding.

'You took it all like a good girl,' he growls and, bringing his mouth to my nipple, bites it.

'You fucking animal,' I curse and it is like playing with fire. The beast inside him takes over. He withdraws from my pussy and slams back in so hard my breasts quake, and my whole body shunts upwards. I feel the jolt in my bones. It is like being drilled into. I grunt.

He rams into me again, but this time I am ready for him and I enjoy it.

'Is that all you got?' I goad, squeezing the splendid thickness inside me.

It isn't. He turns my insides into molten lava. I think my clit is alive and will burst into flames. Trapped under this giant, I fucking lose it. Ferociously, I jam my hips upwards, tangle my legs around his ass, and scream like a foghorn as he continues to thrust into me.

When it is over, I gaze up at him mistily. His cock is buried so deep inside me I think I own it. It must be mine. It is a shock when he pulls out of me suddenly. He releases my hands and falls on his back on the bed.

'Now ride me,' he orders.

I cannot wait to fulfill that command. I crawl to him, greedily lower myself onto the glorious pillar of hard meat and lock my muscles around the throbbing goodness. Impaled on his cock, my body sighs with possessive pleasure. This man was made for me. I lean forward to balance myself and begin to move on his thick shaft. Each hard slam makes him shoot deeper into me.

'That's it. Ride me hard.'

He comes like a raging bull, his body heaving, his head thrown back, his lips curled back in a snarl, and his eyes glazed and unseeing. I ride him through it all. When he stops exploding and becomes still, I can see the wavy heat rising from our joined flesh. I rub my pussy on him restlessly. I don't want his cock out of my body.

'You want more, Princess?'

'I do,' I say, but in fact, I feel completely drained and sleepy.

He holds me and rolls himself so we are both lying on our sides facing each other. Slowly, he slips out of me. My legs feel cramped and stiff and I straighten them with a sigh.

He touches my hair. 'So silky,' he mutters.

My eyes droop closed for a second before I realize that I am falling asleep. I force them open and look at him. It is astonishing how awake and alert he seems to be.

'Aren't you sleepy?' I ask.

'Nope. I have a high metabolic rate. I don't tire fast. In fact, I hardly ever sleep.' He eases off the condom, ties it, and chucks it over the edge of the bed.

'Really? That's amazing.'

'It's not all it's cracked up to be. I spend too many nights when everyone else is asleep wandering around like some night creature.'

'Is that why they call you The Bat? Because you're up all night.'

He gives me an odd look, as if he is deciding what to tell me. 'No, that's not why.'

I get up on my elbow and look at him curiously. 'Why then?'

In one smooth move he is on his haunches and has pulled me upright on the bed. We stand facing each other. 'Because when I was 15 I didn't know how to control my rage or my power and that made me fierce and vicious. This is how I fought then.'

He tucks his chin down to his chest, rounds his shoulders, and moves his fists as if he is throwing punches to the sides of my body. They only touch my body, but I get a measure of how lightning-fast his delivery is, and how impossible it must be to try and evade them if he was doing it for real. In seconds, I feel disorientated and I don't resist when he grabs my shoulders, swooping down to touch his open mouth to the side of my neck. He lifts his head and stares at me.

'I bit them hard enough to draw blood. At the end of every fight, my mouth was always dripping with their blood and sometimes I even spat out flesh.'

I stand frozen with shock. 'Why were you so angry?'

Something flashes in his eyes. Something that hurt him badly. It shocks me to see him so vulnerable. And then a veil comes over his eyes. He had accidently revealed too much. 'I didn't bring you here to talk. You're here to fuck and to suck cock,' he says, pushing my shoulders downwards.

I get on my knees. His cock is already rock hard, but just a moment ago I saw something in his eyes. Some terrible pain.

'It's a nice cock. I'll enjoy sucking it,' I say, softly looking up at him.

I lean forward and lick the smooth head. He rakes his fingers through my hair, fists them, and fucks my mouth as if I am a prostitute he picked up on a street corner.

But I understood, even when I was getting on my knees, that it is the hurt, the terrible hurt that I reminded him of that is driving him.

He comes in my mouth without asking if he can.

I get it. He has just made me submit. Made me swallow his cum. He has owned me. I look up at him, my mouth still full of his softening flesh. His shoulders heave. He pulls out of me, crouches down, and we stare at each other. And I know that something has changed.

'I have to leave,' I say.

'Stay the night.'

'I can't. Dominic is taking me out to breakfast.'

'Sorry, I can't let you go just yet. I haven't had enough of you yet.'

'I'm too sore, BJ.'

'I know,' he says softly, his voice husky. 'I won't hurt you.'

I feel my stomach lift.

He puts me on my back, pins me to the bed with his body, and kisses my eyes. What he does afterwards can only be called a worship of my body with his tongue and mouth. He covers every inch of me kissing, sucking, licking, nipping, biting. Neck, hands, fingers, legs, toes, breasts, nipples, stomach, hips, back, buttocks, asshole, and—finally, finally when I am shivering with arousal —clit.

The result of so much attention is an orgasm like I've never had. The kind where there are stars at the back of your eyelids and you really think you are going to pass out, or perhaps you even actually pass out. No wonder the French call it *la petite mort*, the little death. It is so consuming and powerful I feel almost melancholy and tears slip out of my eyes.

He looks at them curiously, bending his head to lick them.

The gesture is so innocent, so without guile that it makes me feel unreal. At that surreal moment I believe myself to be merely a reflection on a shiny surface or part of a dream. It is in the play of light from the flames in the fireplace on his face that pulls me back. I see him for what he really is. A totally misunderstood, half-man, half-beast, hiding a suffering heart. And I feel as protective over him as a mother bear of her cubs. I could never let anyone hurt him. And I know, in this moment, that I must never, never bring harm to him. I must guard him from the wrath of my family.

I touch his scar and he flinches.

'What happened?'

'Someone bit me,' he says quietly, but I know it was not just anyone. The scar is still alive in his mind. And sometimes when I look at him, it even seems so to me.

'A scar is a special thing. It means you were stronger than whatever tried to hurt you.'

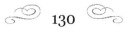

His eyes widen. He stares at me in wonder.

'What?'

He shakes his head. 'You're just different than what I thought you would be.'

I smile. 'What did you think I'd be?'

He shakes his head again and looks away. 'Not like this.' He sits up. 'Are you hungry?'

'Starving actually.'

'Come on. I'll feed you and then take you home.'

We dress quickly as if we are leaving the scene of a crime. I have a great desire to stroke his cheek and make it better. But what am I making better? We have nothing but sex between us. There can be nothing between us, but secret passion. He looks at me, his stance, waiting, watching, patient.

I tie my skirt over my shirt, shrug on my jacket, and slip into my shoes. 'Ready,' I declare.

He takes me to a Chinese restaurant, one of these places that stays open all night. He orders what seems to be the entire menu.

'Are you really going to eat all that?'

'I burned a lot of calories tonight,' he says with a grin.

The food starts arriving almost immediately. He has ordered all kinds of food, but I feel full after a helping of Kung Po chicken and ginger prawns on half a bowl of rice. It is actually too late to eat.

Feeling lethargic and satiated and happy, I lean my chin on my hand and watch with sleepy detachment as he goes through the pile of food. In the car, I yawn and lean my head back against the head rest. He turns towards me.

'Meet me for dinner tomorrow?'

'I can't. I have to be in bed early. I have a job interview on Wednesday.'

'I'll call you and we'll meet for lunch instead,' he suggests.

The feeling of contentment disappears. 'Let me call you,' I say quickly.

'Why?'

I bite my lip. 'Jake doesn't approve of me dating you.'

He leans away from me, his eyes grim. 'I'm not going to sneak around behind anyone's back.'

I feel the happiness ebbing away. 'I was using the word approve euphemistically. He promised all-out war.'

He runs his hand through his hair. 'Let me talk to him.'

'No, don't. Please. Don't. It's better if you don't.'

'I'm not afraid of Jake, Layla. I'll fight anybody for what's mine.'

I stare at him in shock as a flare of pure joy zings through my body. 'I'm yours?'

'Yeah, you're fucking mine. And I don't take kindly to anyone standing between me and my woman.'

'He thinks you're a drug dealer and he wants better for me.'

'Too fucking bad. I don't tell him how to live his life. If I want you, I'll fucking have you.'

'Maybe if you weren't dealing in drugs, Jake wouldn't be so against our relationship?'

He looks at me. 'I do what I do because this is what I am. This is what I know and this is what I am good at. I won't change for Jake.'

I sigh. 'But what you're doing is dangerous. It's only a matter of time before you end up behind bars.

He shakes his head. 'You have to trust me. I deal only in class 3 grass where the sentence is light and I have set it up in such a way that it never passes through my hands.'

I feel suddenly heavy hearted and tearful. Jake is right. What future is there for me with someone like him? He won't change.

I drop my face. 'Anyway, what we have might burn out quickly and we would have upset everyone for nothing.'

He grabs my chin. 'You don't get it. I don't give a shit about upsetting everyone

else. You're mine and the sooner everyone knows it the better.'

'Don't push me, BJ. I love my family and I don't want to hurt them. I'll tell Jake when the time is right. You have to trust me that I know my brother better than you.'

His jaw is set hard. A pulse throbs in it like a heart. 'Don't delay it too long, or I'll have to take it into my own hands.'

EIGHTEEN

Layla

'**D**id you sleep last night?' Dominic asks.

I flush. 'Why do you ask?' I question defensively. We are standing outside my flat in the weak morning sunshine.

'You always have blue shadows under your eyes when you don't sleep well.'

'Oh! Yeah, I didn't sleep too well last night. Just a bit worried about my interview tomorrow, I guess,' I lie.

'If that asshole doesn't give you the job, just let me know and I'll send a couple of boys around to smash up his offices.'

I give him a dirty look and he grins.

'That might have been funny if it had come from Shane. From you it's just downright scary,' I say, getting into his brand new BMW i8.

He laughs and I join in. I love it when Dominic laughs. It changes his whole face.

The car is filled with the scent of new leather and the strawberry air freshener that hangs from the rearview mirror. The engine roars aggressively to life and I settle back to enjoy a wild ride. My brother drives like a mad man.

He says he wants to try out his new chef, so he takes me to breakfast at a wine bar he has recently acquired. It's an old railway station that has been converted for commercial purposes. It still has the metal finials and a platform in the middle. He has named it Applegate Station. The décor is a cross between eclectic and sophisticated with a painted piano, French farmhouse style rustic accessories, chintz upholstery with peacocks and bright foliage, and dark wooden floors. The overall effect is effortless chic.

'What do you want to eat?'

He orders scrambled eggs with smoked salmon and I tell the waiter to double the order.

People are terrified of Dominic because he has such a ready and explosive temper, but I know he is the only one who can stand up to Jake if necessary. So I decide to very gently put out some feelers.

'I was out with Ria last night,' I say stirring sugar into my coffee, 'and I was curious. What was the feud with the Pilkingtons actually about?'

'I don't know. I don't think anyone knows. It was centuries ago. These things start for small matters and carry on through the generations. Each generation hating each other without knowing why.'

'I see. So now our families are friends?'

He takes a sip of orange juice and studies me over his glass. 'I guess so.'

I have to be careful. Dominic is a hot head but he is very intelligent. Very quick to catch on.

'Do we do business with the Pilkingtons?'

'Not really. We have our territories clearly drawn up so there are no misunderstandings. BJ doesn't mess with us and we don't mess with him.'

'So why did Jake and BJ fight then?'

'It was a misunderstanding.'

'Right.' I pause. 'So technically there's no reason why our families shouldn't do business or socialize?'

'Technically? No.' His voice has become still and his face watchful.

'Well, I think you've done a fine job with this place. It's beautiful. Ah... and here comes the food.'

The waiter puts the food on the table. After a flurry of questions about whether we want black pepper or more drinks, we are alone again. I pick up my knife and fork. '*Bon appetito*,' I wish heartily.

'Layla.' Dominic's voice is too quiet.

I put my fork and knife down and slowly lift my eyes up to his.

He is staring at me with disbelief. 'Who did you really go out with last night?'

I lean back against the bright peacock and foliage upholstered chair. 'BJ,' I admit quietly.

His hand comes crashing down on the table. The cutlery and plates jump. I jump. I have never seen Dominic get angry with me.

My hand covers my mouth.

'Fuck!' he swears loudly.

I stare at him. He puts his palm over one eye. 'What the fuck, Layla?'

'Please,' I beg. 'Please don't tell Jake.'

At the mention of Jake's name, Dominic erupts into another litany of loud curses. Fortunately, the place is not yet open to the public. I can hear the staff in the bar scurrying out to the back.

I sit it out until he gets a hold of himself. 'How far has the relationship gone?'

'I've only met him a few times. It's not really a relationship. It's just a sex thing.'

'Don't fucking tell me that! I'm your fucking brother.'

'Sorry,' I apologize quickly.

'BJ! Why? Why on earth did you have to choose him? He's such a fucking dog. He's gone through *all* the women in Shane's club.' He stares at me. 'Every fucking one.'

I look down. I know I should be ashamed. I should be mortified that I've given myself to a man who is so obviously a man-whore, but I'm not. And that thought gives me sudden strength. I won't sit here and let my brother abuse BJ. I have something with BJ and I don't want to be disloyal to that thing, whatever it is. I reach out my hand and place it on my brother's arm. It pulls him out of his rage.

'He's not like what you think.'

My brother groans. 'How can you even say that? He's got you going behind all our backs and lying! Shit! He's havin' a laugh at our family's expense. I thought he was more honorable than that!'

I flush to the roots of my hair. 'It's not his fault. He wanted to confront Jake, but I begged him not to. It's the wrong time. Jake is so happy at the moment. In less than a month he is going to be a dad. I don't want to spoil it for him.'

I see Dominic's expression change and I press my advantage. 'Besides, if BJ is the dog you say he is, it will all be over in the next couple of weeks. Why worry and upset Jake unnecessarily?'

'You deserve better than that barbarian, Layla.' He looks sad when he says it.

'It's just an experience, Dom. I'm not planning to marry him or have a family with him. I'm all grown up now and I'm just spreading my wings, living my life.'

'If he fucking hurts you ...'

'I am not going to get hurt. I'm going in with my eyes wide open. But if I do get hurt, then I'll pick myself up, dust myself off, and I'll be wiser for it. I won't shame our family.'

'I'll give you until the baby is born. If you're not finished spreading your wings by then I'm telling Jake,' he says sternly.

'Thank you. I know it will have died away by then.'

'It better fucking have,' he says morosely.

After that we eat our breakfast, but my news has put Dominic in a foul mood and by the time he drops me off I too have been affected by it.

I call BJ.

He answers on the first ring. There is tension in his voice. 'Hi. Everything OK?'

'Not really. I stupidly asked Dom a few questions about the feud and you, and he immediately guessed. So I had to tell him. He didn't react very well, but he did promise not to interfere and to let me tell Jake when I'm ready.'

'Want to do lunch?'

'Yeah, but let's go somewhere no one knows us.'

NINETEEN

Layla

I have my stockinged feet up on the radiator and the radio is on as we drive away from London to BJ's country house. Outside, the rain is lashing down in sheets making visibility poor. It makes me feel we are in a bubble. *Lost Frequencies* comes on.

'This is my most favorite song in the whole wide world,' I tell him and turn it up as loud as it will go.

He smiles.

My lips are painted red and I feel happy. The kind of happy that makes you feel like you can jump up and touch the ceiling. When you think you love the whole world and everyone in it because you are so happy.

The electric gates open and we drive into Silver Lee. It is only two o'clock, but it is already dark and all the lights have been lit. BJ opens the door and I precede him.

'Is no one in?'

'No, I asked my housekeeper to make himself scarce until later tonight.'

I grin. 'So we are totally alone?'

'Not quite. There is someone I have to introduce you to.'

I raise my eyebrows.

'He's a bit of an old fart and doesn't like people, but he's kind of important to me so let's see what you make of each other.'

'OK.'

We walk down through the house with its curving glass frontage. A storm is raging outside. He pauses by a door. 'He can be quite foul mouthed,' he warns.

Then he opens the door and a nasal voice screeches, 'Did you fuck him?' My mouth drops open. BJ makes an after-you gesture with his hand. 'Bitch, better have my money. Bitch better. Bitch better. Pay me what you owe me.' I enter the room and there is no one in there. There's just a grey parrot with a red tail.

'Meet Jeremy Thomas,' BJ says walking towards the bird. He holds his hand under it. 'Step up,' he says and the bird climbs on to his hand and looks at me with its head cocked to one side. 'Cunt.'

I laugh. 'Did your bird just call me a cunt?'

'Yeah, I forgot to say he's a bit of a misogynist. My mother hates him.'

'Has he called her one too?'

'I'm afraid so. He used to belong to a Jamaican pimp so he generally has a very bad opinion of women and he's always asking them for money.'

'Give Jeremy a nut. Give Jeremy a nut,' the bird squawks.

'What kind of a bird is he?'

'An African Grey.'

'And how on earth did you get him?'

'His owner owed me money and had to leave the country in a hurry. So I took the bird.'

Jeremy fixes me with a belligerent eye and flaps his wings. 'You're wet.'

I gasp.

BJ turns to me with a glimmer of laughter in his eyes. 'It's not what you think. He just wants a bath.'

I laugh.

'Want a cookie.'

BJ gives him something from his pocket and the bird holds it in his claws and eats it.

'Oh BJ. I think he's gorgeous.'

144

BJ grins happily and there is nothing to outshine his smile. I about melt into a puddle right there and then.

'God only knows why I care so much for this stupid bird,' he says.

'You're a wimp,' Jeremy says and begins to laugh like a human.

It is funny and we both laugh.

'Kiss. Oops, bad birdie. Bite the dog. Bad dog.'

'How old is he?'

'Not sure, but older than you and me. He's maybe 40.'

'Wow. Can he fly?'

'Give me the money, bitch,' the bird squawks.

'Yup, he can fly.'

'Do you take him outside?'

'I have in the past, but he doesn't really seem to like it.'

I watch Jeremy get a bath. It's the cutest thing ever. It is fun and we both laugh. I look at BJ with his bird and I can hardly believe that this is the same aggressive fighting monster I saw in the pit.

I offer Jeremy a nut. He takes it from me and quickly flutters away screeching, 'Where's my money, bitch.'

I laugh and BJ catches me by the waist. I look up at him, tall and broad-shouldered, and the laughter dies in my throat.

'Time my cock was inside you,' he says.

I hop on to his body and wrap my legs around his hips. 'Carry me to your bed and ravish me then,' I whisper daringly.

We go up the stairs and he opens the door to the bedroom where I had received my spanking. He puts me at the edge of the bed. Outside the wind howls. Inside we are absolutely silent. I cannot even hear my own heartbeat. The only sound is the fire crackling in the fireplace.

He starts off by kissing me. By the time he raises his mouth I am totally nude.

'That's a clever trick. Now show me my cock,' I whisper hoarsely.

He throws aside his t-shirt and unbuttons his trousers. I drink in the inked, tanned skin, the barely leashed strength in his coiled muscles and follow the line of straight black hair on its epic journey down to his crotch. The last scrap of cloth slides to the floor and I fix my gaze on his cock. Have me with a side order of caviar, or a maraschino cherry and two scoops of ice cream, or just me on my own, but fucking eat me, it screams aggressively.

I *love* his raging cock.

I grab his hips and slowly slide my puckered mouth over the thick roll of meat. He groans with pleasure. The heat of his lust flows from him onto my skin. I love sucking his cock. I'll make all the other women who have taken him into their mouths a memory that never was. It is a lazy, dreamlike thought.

 146

Outside the storm passes. The sky becomes milky white, shadows move, but I do not stop. Every time he is about to come, I pause, I change my rhythm. He hisses with frustration. I understand. It's annoying. But there is a point to it all. My lips grow as numb, but I do not stop. As if sucking his cock is an old tradition that can bring bad luck if broken.

But he has other ideas.

He seizes my head, fully determined that I will no longer have the reins, and starts thrusting lustily towards his climax. I taste the salt in my mouth and jerk my head back so his cum sprays onto my face, my open mouth, my chin, and my throat. There is nothing he has done to another woman that he cannot do to me. When the last drop has been squeezed onto me I slip my tongue out of my mouth and slowly lick his cum from my lips.

He smears the rest on my face, neck and breasts.

Then he pushes me onto my back and presses his naked flank into my softness, crushing it beautifully, and thrusts into my body as it arches up to receive him. The sensation is magic. My loins ache. My insides feel raw. A gasp. A cry. A stiffening. His muscles strain and ripple urgently. We move together, slick and sliding against each other. My breath comes faster as his cock swells inside me. The whole time his gaze never leaves mine, his eyes smoldering and rapt. The moments lengthen into technicolor dreams: rich like wine. I sigh at his gentle hands, his velvet mouth.

Afterwards, I slip on his t-shirt and we drink apple mojitos. He is funny. I laugh. We have sex on the floor. Then we drink more mojitos and eat cold chicken and popcorn. I feel myself become lazily drunk.

'You up for a fuck?' I ask. There is a definite slur in my voice. An elongation of the vowels.

'Is Fukushima leaking radiation?'

I fling off his t-shirt and hair trailing down my naked back, crawl around the food towards him.

He puts a dark hand on my pale exposed shoulder.

I push him to the ground and climb atop him. His strong hands curl around my ribs to keep my body steady as I impale myself on his cock. I know I'm tipsy and without a steady rhythm. Despite that, we come quickly. I lie on his body and listen to the dull beat of his heart. I love simply having him inside me.

'I could fall asleep like this,' I whisper.

'Get on your hands and knees, woman.'

Hours later, the fire has burned down to embers and ashes. I lie weary and trembling beside him in the dark. I reach out a hand and touch him, a gesture that is both a question and reverent. My eyes are wide and filled with a strange new perspective, an awareness, an impossible intensity, as if I have never been truly or fully alive before.

'I have to get back to London soon.'

He turns towards me, his face drugged and slack with desire. 'Not yet. I've not had enough of you.'

'Ahhhhh,' I gasp, my juices splashing into his mouth.

TWENTY

Layla

'**I** got the job,' I crow into the phone.

He laughs. A good sound.

'You are now talking to a member of Vincent & Prestige's Studio's team of interior designers. I start my first design and fit-out assignment on Monday!'

'Want to celebrate over lunch?'

I feel the disappointment inside my body, like a wave passing through. 'I can't.

I'm going shopping with my sister-in-law. We're buying baby stuff.'

'How's Lily?'

'She's quietly freaking out after convincing Jake that she should have a totally natural childbirth in their bathtub. She's actually going to give birth without an epidural! Apparently she's going to be sucking on sugar pills the whole time. I told her I think she's bananas. When I have a baby I want to be put out. And I don't mean just an epidural. I mean general anesthetic. I don't want to know nothing! Nada. I want to wake up to my husband holding a pink baby all clean and wrapped up in blankets.'

The silence on the other end is so thick you could have spread it on a slice of bread. Then it hits me how I must sound to him. A crazy woman banging on about babies three days after having sex with him. And with him being a player—yeah, even then I resisted the words junkyard dog.

'Thank God it will be at least ten years before I am in such a position,' I rush into the treacle of silence.

'We should celebrate your job offer,' he says evenly.

I breathe a sigh of relief. 'Yeah, we should,' I agree.

'Where do you want to go?' he asks.

My response is immediate. No need to think about it. 'Silver Lee.'

'Don't you want to go somewhere nice? It's a celebration, after all.'

'Nope. I still haven't had a proper tour of your house, remember?'

Strike two. I hear his reluctance, like sandpaper on my skin. He doesn't want to give me a tour. Why on earth not? 'If you don't want to it's OK.' Oh my God! I am becoming a doormat.

There is a pause. Then. 'All right. I'll show you around. Pick you up at 3:00?'

'See you then.'

I slip into the passenger seat of BJ's carbon-edition Aston Martin, close the door, and turn toward him. Wow! He's rocking a sexy five o'clock shadow, which makes him look all moody and brooding. His eyes graze over me slowly, but being so dark they give nothing away.

'Hi,' I greet breathlessly.

He leans over and kisses me. I'll say this for him: the man can kiss. In seconds I want to throw my arms around his neck, curl my fingers in his hair, and climb over to his side of the car to lower myself on to his thick cock. My skin tingles. My head starts buzzing. My hand strays to his hard chest.

'What was that for?' I whisper, when he breaks away.

His eyes are smoky with desire. He places his finger on my lower lip and drags

it along my skin. His voice drops to a faux whisper that caresses my skin. 'Because you're so damn beautiful.'

I drop my eyes and go all hot and red with sheer happiness.

He places a finger under my chin and lifts my face. 'Isn't that what all the boys who aren't afraid of your brother tell you?'

My stomach flips. 'I think there are more boys afraid of my brother than you think.'

'Since I'm not in the firing line yet, let me tell you, Layla. You're one hell of a beauty.'

'You're not so bad looking yourself,' I say shyly.

'Me? I'm an ugly mug. You, you're another matter. You truly are the beginning of intoxication.'

'That reminds me, how is it you know so much about my name. Even I thought Layla meant of the night in Arabic.'

'Because I researched it, Princess.'

'Is that why you bought a tiepin with the word Layla on it?'

His face closes over.

I frown. 'What?'

'Nothing.' He turns away and starts the engine. 'So Lily is having a homebirth. When?'

'Well,' I say settling myself into the seat. 'The baby is not due for another three weeks.'

'And Jake is OK with a homebirth?'

'Oh, he didn't like it one bit at first, but being the total control freak that he is, he went out and offered the best midwife in England so much money she is going to uproot her entire family, 3 kids no less, to go and stay at his house two weeks before the baby is due. From what I understand, the poor woman will be virtually a prisoner until the baby is born. Of course he's also hired a whole medical team to be on standby just in case there's any kind of complication.'

He laughs. 'That sounds more like him.' He sobers suddenly. 'When do you plan to tell him about us?'

It is my turn to sober up. 'I want to tell him, but he's so happy at the moment. In fact, I don't think I've ever seen him so full of laughter. Can you believe he sings to his baby?'

He turns to look at me briefly, his eyebrows raised.

'I just don't want to spoil this time for him. I'll tell him after the baby is born.' I pause for a second. Then, I don't know why, perhaps I am testing him, I add, 'If we are still together by then.'

His face registers no change, but his hands tighten on the wheel. 'OK,' he says tightly. 'We wait until after the baby is born, but if I am in a position where he asks me outright I'm not going to lie.'

'That's fair enough.'

After that we talk of things outside of us. Some of it is light and easy and I laugh a lot, but I come to realize quickly that BJ sees everything from a totally different perspective than me. A much darker, more cynical perspective. He is my total opposite in every way. We disagree on almost all the important aspects of life. He seems to be without the usual social pretensions that normal people indulge in. To start with, he doesn't have a Facebook page. He thinks all social media is narcissism gone berserk. He is of the opinion that only birds should tweet. Having 865 Internet friends is ludicrous. And wait for it ... he has never taken a selfie!

He says he will go back to church again when someone explains where black people came from since Adam and Eve were both lily white. He believes that people should not be trusted since the strongest human traits—greed, jealousy, envy, cruelty—are inborn and already active even in children. Humans have to be taught kindness, generosity, patience, and goodness. BJ believes those traits can only be a thin veneer for the real truth, a cauldron of negative emotions.

'So you don't trust me?' I ask him, my voice is light, my manner is flirtatious, but in fact I am really curious as to what he will say.

He throws a brief glance at me. 'Where does your mother think you are now?'

'With Maddy,' I say slowly.

'Have I answered your question?'

'Is there no one you trust?'

'Jeremy. I trust him.'

'That's sad, BJ.'

He shrugs carelessly. 'Save your sympathy. I set it up like this because I like it this way.'

'BJ, isn't your mother alive?'

'Yeah.'

'And you don't trust your own mother?'

'Don't get me wrong. I love my mother. I'd do anything for her but no, she hasn't done much to inspire my trust.'

'My God. What kind of childhood did you have?'

He gives me a sideways glance. 'It wasn't like yours.'

'So you've never trusted anyone in your life?'

'I trusted my father.'

'Why?'

'Because he always showed me his real face. At all times I knew exactly what he was and what I could expect from him.'

Then he is turning into Silver Lee. We go into the house and it is silent, but an amazing lunch has been set out on the dining table. It is almost like being in a fairy tale. Like in Beauty and the Beast when the father finds the deserted palace and a table set with a princely meal.

There is a note on the table. BJ picks it up and reads it.

I am so caught up in the Beauty and the Beast scenario I think that the note might be important. 'What does it say?' I ask curiously.

He passes it to me.

There is a tall jug of mojitos
waiting in the fridge.
Marcel

He looks at me, sexy smile on his face. 'Well, what do you want to do first? Eat or fuck?'

If any other man had said that I'd have slapped him and called him a coarse jerk. But BJ, he's the shining hero in the movie I'm directing, producing, and starring in.

And God! I want him.

'Fuck,' I say with half-closed, sultry eyes. Turning, I begin to walk away while undressing at the same time. The dark green top goes over my head and on the floor. My bra follows. I turn around and he is just behind me, staring at my breasts possessively. The desire to press my naked body against him is astonishingly strong, white-knuckle strong.

I lie on a long lilac couch and shimmy out of my skirt and panties. I am suddenly almost feverish with need. Daringly I open my legs wide. He gets down on his haunches and slides his hand up my leg, towards my

distended, swollen clitoris. With precise, knowing strokes he rubs the flesh around it. His carnal expertise is irresistible.

I squirm and whimper.

It has never crossed my mind that I would ever be so wild for a man.

He brings his head closer and I prepare for his tongue. Instead a flow of warm air hits my exposed sex.

'Ah,' I cry at the exquisitely delicate sensation. Like a fine wine or the faint earthy flavor of truffle shavings on a plate of buttery pasta. My eyes close to fully savor it. When his silky tongue touches my clit it is unexpected and shockingly intense. My body arches like a bow. He licks the pulsing flesh like a kitten. He slides his fingers deeper inside me and pumps them furiously. My body heats up and sweat dampens my skin. I grasp his hair and curl my legs around his large body, the way he taught me to.

'Please,' I beg.

He lifts his head and unlocking my legs, opens me wide. He stands and looks down at me splayed and ready for him. With heavy-lidded eyes he starts to undress. He discards his pants and my gaze moves to the well-defined, hard bulge in his white briefs. The thick mushroom head is already poking out of the top of his underwear. He stops. My eyes move up to his and hot blood rushes up my throat to be caught looking at his erection so hungrily. I have never stared at a man like this. Not ever.

He fits a rubber on himself and, putting his hands on either side of me, mounts me. He pounds me hard a few times. There is something frenzied and electric about the urgency of his thrusts. I know then that he cannot wait any longer. I milk the cream of his body with my own and he explodes, his head thrown back and utterly silent.

For seconds his face is buried in my breasts. He might even have gently sucked my nipple, I am in a daze of contentment. Then he rouses himself and, looking into my eyes, brings me to climax.

'You're beautiful when you come,' he whispers. His face is flushed and his eyes are the softest black.

Afterwards, we eat, but I find I have hardly any appetite. Every time his eyes rest on me, I feel my lack of underwear, how wet I am, and how much I long to have him back inside me.

Maddy's call interrupts our total absorption with each other. She tells me my mother is looking for me. I didn't hear my phone while we were having sex. I look up at BJ. His eyes are expressionless. He listens to me call my mother and lie about where I am and what I am doing since I am not with Maddy after all. It is easy to lie to Ma. She isn't expecting me to. I end the call and face him.

'I'll get the mojitos,' he says and walks away. Strange. He is the criminal and yet he is the more honorable of us.

TWENTY-ONE

BJ

When I come back with the drinks she has slipped into my t-shirt and is seated in a recess of one of the tall windows. Twelve feet of pale yellow glow from the wintry evening sun falls on her wonderful, thick hair and tinges it with a light that I have only seen in paintings from the great Dutch masters. Perhaps a Rembrandt.

A living spectacle.

She turns to look at me and smiles a smile that nearly knocks me backwards. I have been with countless women, all of

them beautiful, vibrant and sexy. But she makes them all pale into insignificance. The thought is terrifying and beautiful. Never again will I be with a woman who can satisfy me the way she does.

I stand over her and hold out the drink. She takes it with both hands. She is the first woman who has persuaded me to drink a mojito. And now I fucking like it!

'You promised me a tour,' she says. There is a hint of laughter in her voice. I love that about her. Only children and the truly innocent have that. I don't really want to show her my sex room, but she stands and holds out her hand. So we go through the entire house until we get to the sex room. I open the door and she goes in, flicks the switch, and the disco lights come on. She touches the switch beside it and Kanye West's *Gold Digger* fills the room. For a few seconds she says nothing.

Fuck. Fuck. Fuck.

I see what I have never seen before. I see how bad it really is. How stupid and vulgar and truly ugly and cringingly embarrassing it is. What was I thinking bringing her here? She is too grand for this gaudiness. I want to usher her out immediately and rip it all up.

Slowly she turns to look up at me and I swear I stop breathing. Her shoulders come up as she is about to be sick, but instead of being sick, her mouth trembles. I'll be damned. She is trying not to laugh! I don't

know what is worse. That she should think it hideous or laughable.

'Come on, let's go,' I say brusquely.

She grabs my arm. 'No, no, I think it's great. Really.'

I look at her curiously. Is she serious?

She gestures around her. 'Everything all at once like this. I've just never seen it before. That's all.' She becomes serious. 'But in fact, I should have expected it. It's you. You say it like it is. There's no pretense. No veneer of what is socially acceptable. It is what it is. A room for sex. If someone gets brought here, they'll know without any doubt what you want from them.'

She walks into the room, heads for the bed, and sits on the edge. She pats the space next to her and strangely I don't feel my cock rise to the occasion. Instead I feel a horrible feeling in my gut that even just sitting on that bed would somehow contaminate her.

She pats it again and smiles slowly.

I walk over and sit next to her. She climbs into my lap. My cock forgets its reservations and stirs to life.

'I was thinking of dismantling this room,' I say.

'Why? I like it. We can have funny sex here.'

'Funny sex?'

She draws away from me. 'Yeah, like when you bang your head on the headboard, laugh, and then have sex anyway.'

163

'Right.'

'You've *never* had funny sex?' she asks incredulously.

'I guess not.' And judging from her description it's not something I'm going to rush to try either.

She tilts her head to one side and I feel something inside me melt. Shit, I'm done for. This woman has me all tied up in knots. She tries to tickle my midriff. I'm not ticklish. Her fingers move to my armpits. I shrug. 'Sorry.'

'You're really not ticklish?'

Her expression of incredulity is adorable and I laugh.

'There you go,' she says laughing and pushes me backwards towards the bed. She puts her palms on either side of my face and brings her open mouth to mine. Ah, the kiss. This is not me kissing her. This is her kissing me. Soft. Her mouth is so soft and sweet. Smelling of mojitos and sugar and Layla. My Layla.

It seems that I like funny sex after all.

What part of her flesh have I not tasted?
Her smell adheres to my hands and nails.

TWENTY-TWO

Layla

'Congratulate me. I'm an aunt,' I shout excitedly into the phone.

'Brilliant. How's the mother?' BJ asks.

'She's fine. Now ask me how the father is.'

He laughs. 'How's Jake?'

'Freaking out. You should see him. He's so crazy about his baby he won't even let anyone else carry her. I had to elbow him out of the way to even look at her.'

'So everyone is happy.'

'Yeah, everyone is really happy. I'll send you a picture of her. She's got hairy ears, but ma says even I had hairy ears when I was born and it will fall off.'

'You still have hairy ears.'

'Quit it or I'll send you the pictures where she still has cottage cheese all over her body.'

He bursts out laughing.

'Layla,' my mother calls from behind me.

'Got to go, Maddie, I'll speak to you later, OK?' I say and quickly cut the connection.

'Are you staying for dinner?' my mother asks. She is so happy she is glowing like it's Christmas morning. This is her first grandchild and an event she has been praying for ever since Jake turned 21.

I touch her hand. 'Might not be a good idea, Ma. I have to work tomorrow. I'll come back on the weekend.'

'Are you leaving now then?'

'Yeah, before the traffic gets heavy.'

'Do you want me to make you a sandwich before you go?'

'No, I'll go and say goodbye to Jake and Lily and be off.'

'Lily is sleeping. Poor thing is exhausted.'

'Fine. I'll just go say goodbye to my brother and my niece then.'

'Come and see me in the kitchen before you go. I've made some food for you to take back.'

'OK,' I say and run up the stairs of Jake's house. I stand at the door of the nursery transfixed by the sight of Jake bent over Liliana's cradle.

'Hey,' I say softly and he looks up, his expression soft.

'Hey,' he whispers.

I walk up to the cot. He is gently stroking her cheek with his finger.

'Congratulations, Jake. Other than the hairy ears she's beautiful.'

He looks up at me, a huge, stupid grin on his face. 'She is, isn't she.'

Suddenly I feel an overwhelming wave of love for my brother. All these years he never had anything for himself. To call his own. Always he was fighting all our battles. I blink back the tears.

His eyes narrow. 'What's wrong?'

'Nothing's wrong. Everything's just perfect.'

He nods. 'Are you going back to London now?'

'Yeah. The traffic won't be so bad now.'

'Why don't you stay a bit longer and let Shane drive you back?'

I shake my head. 'Then you'll just have the hassle of sending my car back to me.'

He frowns. 'It's no trouble.'

I smile softly. 'No, it is trouble for you. I'll be back for the weekend.'

'All right. Drive safely.'

'I will.'

That's the thing about Jake. Even at a time like this he is worrying about me. I hug him tightly and go down to the kitchen. My mother is putting together plastic containers of food into two carrier bags. The containers are labeled so I know exactly what's in them. Dom is sitting at the table finishing off a massive bacon and sausage sandwich.

'Are you off?' he asks me.

'Yeah.'

'Didn't you have something else you had to do?' He puts the last bit of the sandwich into his mouth and raises his eyebrows meaningfully.

I glance at my mother, but she is busy washing her hands.

'I'm not doing it today. I'll be back this weekend, I'll do it then.'

My brother wipes his mouth and stands up. 'I'm off then. See you at dinnertime, Ma.' As he passes me he whispers, 'I wouldn't wait beyond the weekend if I were you.'

I watch my brother leave with a heavy heart.

'Put this bag into the fridge and consume it today, tomorrow at the latest,' my mother says. I turn back to her. 'And the other bag, you can freeze it and eat on Thursday and Friday. You'll be back here on Saturday, won't you?'

'Yeah. Thanks.'

 169

'Do you want to take some cake for Maddie too?' my mother asks.

'No, I'll share what I've got with her.'

'All right then,' she says moving towards the fridge.

'Ma,' I say sinking into a chair.

'What?'

'Did you ever think we'd all turn out like this?'

She looks at me. 'Never.'

'What did you think we'd become?'

'I didn't know. I didn't dare dream anything like this. I thought we'd always be struggling,' she says softly.

'You're really proud of Jake, aren't you?'

She is so choked up she can't even speak. Just nods violently, her body clenched tight.

'Me too,' I say.

She comes outside with me, and waves as I drive away. I watch her become smaller in the mirror and I get a horrible cold feeling in my stomach. When I am far enough away, I pull over by the side of the road and call BJ.

'What's up?' he asks immediately.

'Oh, BJ. I don't know how I can ever tell Jake about us.' My voice is shaking.

There is a tense pause. 'Where are you now?' he asks urgently.

'About a mile away from Jake's house.'

'Look, I can be at Silver Lee in about an hour. Do you want to go there and wait for me?'

With all the excitement about the baby, no one will notice my absence so I could even spend the night there and leave very early in the morning for London. 'But what about Marcel?'

'I'll ask him to leave the French doors open for you.'

'OK, I'll see you there in about an hour,' I say.

'Layla.'

'Yeah.'

'We'll figure it out, OK.'

'OK.'

'BJ.'

'Yeah?'

'Nothing. I'll talk to you when I see you.'

I sever the connection and stare at my phone. It seems impossible that I once thought my relationship with BJ would diminish with time. That I had actually told Dom that it was just a sex thing. It's far from just a sex thing. My feelings have grown and grown.

I know BJ likes me. Maybe a lot, but I also know that I can't base my future on that alone. He owns clubs full of beautiful women who are constantly throwing themselves at him. When I am not with him, I sometimes worry. All kinds of thoughts plague me. We haven't promised to be exclusive with each other. Our relationship is like a dirty secret. We never go any place where we could be recognized. No one in his life knows. Even Marcel has never seen me. At least in my life, Maddy and Dominic know. Now that Lily has given birth, I might even tell her and ask her advice.

With a sigh I put my phone back into my purse and start the car. I reach Silver Lee in about 40 minutes. The gates are wide open and I drive through. It is the beginning of spring and there are daffodils all along the road up to the house. It looks beautiful. And somehow that makes me feel sadder. Will I see them next year or the year after? I park my car and walk along the side of the house. One of the French doors is open and I slip in and lock it.

I know Marcel would have taken Jeremy and the house feels silent and totally empty without BJ. My heels are loud on the floor. I go to the kitchen and open the fridge and smile. Marcel made a jar of mojitos before he left. I pour myself a tumbler and go into the vast, open living room. I sit on the long lilac sofa and gaze out into the countryside.

I'm surprised to hear BJ's car roar up the driveway a few minutes later. I put my drink on a nearby table and go to the front door. He opens it as I get there. The moment is rare. I've never opened a door to him before. It's nice. It makes me feel like we are a normal couple.

'You got here fast,' I say softly.

His eyes are dark and searching. 'I drove fast.'

I take a step towards him. He pulls me hard into his arms and kisses me.

'Come on. Marcel has made us mojitos,' I say breathlessly.

He looks down at me and nods.

We go to the kitchen where I pour a glass for him and we walk out together to the sofa. We chink glasses.

'Here's to the new aunt,' he says.

I smile. 'And the new baby.'

'And that,' he adds.

We both take a sip. He eyes me over the rim of his glass. 'My poor Layla,' he says quietly.

'I'm sorry I'm being such a baby, but I can't bear the thought of disappointing them all, especially Jake.'

'He has to know, Layla. Sooner or later. We can't carry on like this.'

'I know. I know. I will.' I drop my face into my hands. 'I just don't want him to hate me.'

'He's not going to hate you. This is your life. Nothing would have stood in the way of him being with Lily. He has no right to stop you from seeing anyone you want to. You're a grown woman.'

'It's just feels as if I have betrayed him.'

'The longer you leave it, the worse the betrayal will be.'

"Maybe I'll tell him after Ella's wedding. You're going too, aren't you?'

He grins. 'Only to look at you.'

I blush. 'Really?'

'Abso-fucking-lutely.'

'Anyway,' I say, suddenly feeling all shy and awkward. 'I'll be staying over at my mother's that night and I'll break it to all of them at the same time.'

'Do you want me to be there?'

'No.' I shiver at the thought. 'Definitely not.'

'OK.' For a moment we are both silent. He takes a sip of his drink. 'Have you heard the story of Layla and Majnun by Nizami?'

I shake my head.

'It's about a moon-princess who was married off by her father to someone other than the man who was desperately in love with her. It resulted in his madness.'

I bow my head. It would be all so different if he wasn't a criminal.

TWENTY-THREE

BJ

'**I** know so little about you, BJ,' Layla complains as she locks her arms around my waist and angles her head back to catch my eyes.

God, she's so fucking sexy, I just want to fuck her every time she comes near me. She's got about ten minutes before I fill that honey mouth of hers full of cock.

'What'd you want to know, Princess?'

'Tell me why you became a criminal?' she asks.

I shrug carelessly. 'Why does anyone?'

She gazes up at me, her beautiful blue eyes narrowed. 'Is it for all the power and respect you command: men shaking in their boots, women worshiping at your feet?'

'I followed in my father's footsteps, Layla,' I tell her. An early memory of my father floats into my mind. He is sitting on a barstool flexing and unflexing his bulging arm muscles just before a fight. There is loud music in the background and on the table in front of him, two pints of Guinness are lined up.

'Your father?' she says softly. 'He must have been quite a character. Your mother showed me her wedding photograph and he looked very handsome. It was so sweet to hear her describe him as a "rakishly dreamy charmer".'

I remember Lenny Pilkington differently. The charm was long gone by the time I knew him, and my young self saw only a giant of a man, with a flattened, boxer's nose, shrewd eyes, and a savage temper. My jaw stiffens unconsciously.

'What's wrong?" Layla frowns.

I block the thoughts immediately. 'Nothing.'

Her eyes narrow suspiciously. 'Did he force you to become a criminal, BJ?' she demands.

I let my facial muscles relax. 'Of course not. I desperately wanted to follow in my father's and my uncles' footsteps. I guess I was impressed by their big, flashy cars and their jacked-up pick-up trucks.'

'So how old were you when you joined them?'

'Eleven.'

Her eyes become saucers. 'Eleven? I was still playing with my dolls when I was eleven.'

Seems so long ago and yet the day I accompanied them on my first job is as vivid as if it happened yesterday.

'You were just a kid. What did they make you do?'

I laugh at her belligerent expression. 'Relax. All I had to do was stand casually outside the gates of an industrial site and hoot twice like an owl if anyone, especially the pigs happened along while my father and two of my uncles filled their truck with scrap metal.'

'I still think you were far too young to be involved in something like that,' she says, her voice full of disapproval. In her world fathers protected their sons.

Strange, even after all these years I still feel the burning need to defend my father. 'The truth is, Layla, it felt fucking great. From that first time I was hooked on the mix of adrenaline and excitement that pumped through my body.'

'What did you guys do with the scrap metal?'

'Dropped it off at my uncle's yard.'

'And after?'

'Afterwards, we drove to the local pub. It was a winter's night and I sat in the beer garden and froze my ass off while my father went in and bought me my first pint of ale. It was fucking terrible, but I drank it all up. I can still remember putting my hands into my armpits and in a drunken haze soaking up their tall tales.

'So the little gangster learned quickly?' she says sadly, dropping her head.

I put my finger under her chin and lift it up. 'Why so sad? My father and uncles prepared me well for a life in the underbelly of society. They taught me to see the world the way it really is. As a sort of jungle where the human race can be divided into three categories: gazelles, lions, and hyenas.'

She looks at me curiously.

'The gazelle is the food of both the lions and hyenas. However, contrary to perceived wisdom, it is not the hyena that steals from the lion, but the lion that will snatch from the mouth of the hyena its hard-won kill. In every place where the lion dominates, the hyena must hunt in packs and use its cunning—or perish all together.

'Am I a gazelle in your world, BJ?'

I shake my head slowly.

'What am I then? Explain the inhabitants of your jungle to me, BJ.'

'The lions are the captains of industry, the bankers, the politicians, the landowners. They wear the mask of nobility. Normal society is represented by the gazelle. They register their births, work all their lives to pay countless taxes, obey even the most idiotic laws, and exist purely to fatten the predator lions. But we Gypsies, you and me, are different. We are the hyenas. Meekness and slavery are not for us. We have, and always will, survive and prosper on our own terms, using our specific talents and wits.

'Now, you sound like Jake. He is always going on about greedy bankers and lying politicians too.'

'That's because he sees through the illusion. And that's why we, Gypsies, have travelled incessantly through the centuries never stopping long enough to put roots. We did it so no one could count us, corral us, educate us, tame us, or enslave us.

She frowns. 'But your father sent you to school?'

'My father was a very shrewd man. He understood the changing times meant we would soon be forced to play their game, anyway. He decided that I would be the first one of us who would have two educations, ours and theirs. So by the time I left school I could read and write as well as the next boy, but my true specialty was numbers. I excelled at them. I didn't even have to try. They just came naturally.'

She smiles for the first time. 'Yeah?'

'Yeah. I was so fucking good I could walk into a scrap yard and in less than thirty seconds, I would have picked out everything of value. I knew where it was going and exactly what it all was worth.'

'You make it sound easy.'

'It was. Money poured in. By the time I was eighteen I got my first shiny new car. A glorious Aston Martin. Paid for in cash.' Those were the days when no one frowned on you for paying in cash. Even now I can feel that rush of pride and possession I felt when I drove that beauty off the forecourt.

'I wish I had been your girl-friend then,' she says softly, and presses her face into my chest.

I don't tell her that was the point in my life when I got into the business of grass. Selling grass to the gazelles.

TWENTY-FOUR

Layla

I wake up early in my bed at my mother's house. The house is quiet. I pull Graystone from his shelf and bury my face against his fur. Today is the day I promised BJ and Dom I will break the news to Jake. And today is also the day I break my great secret to BJ. With a heavy sigh, I get out of bed and open my bedroom door.

'Is that you, Layla?' my mother calls from the kitchen.

'Morning,' I yell back from the top of the stairs.

'Brush your teeth and come down for breakfast. Your ride will be here in an hour.'

Even the thought of breakfast makes me feel sick. 'I don't want breakfast, Ma.'

I hear her footsteps come from the kitchen. Her face appears at the bottom of the stairs. 'Are you sick? Why don't you want breakfast?'

'I just don't feel like it, Ma. I think I'm nervous about today.'

My mother frowns. 'Nervous about today? Why? You've been bridesmaid loads of time. Besides, it's your cousin Ella.'

'Yeah, you're right,' I concede.

'Hurry up then. I'm making you pancakes.'

I get ready and go downstairs. My mother puts a plate with two warm buttery pancakes in front of me. I spread Nutella on one and eat it slowly. It settles like a heavy stone in my stomach. The car arrives and I am borne away to my cousin's house. Fortunately, her house is in such a flurry of hectic activity that I quickly forget my worries and morph into the role of bridesmaid. The flower girls make me laugh. They've overdosed on spray tan and they all look as if they have been thoroughly shaken inside a Doritos bag.

Soon it is time for Ella to get into her wedding dress. It is a monster meringue affair, weighing a staggering 90 pounds.

There are 520 Swarovski crystals on the bodice and more than 100 rings to puff the skirt out to over eight feet in diameter. Someone fits the veil on her head and she turns to us with shining eyes.

'You look like a fairy tale princess,' I tell her. She really does.

'I feel like Cinderella, Sleeping Beauty, and Snow White all rolled into one,' she says with a catch in her voice.

At that moment I feel a faint sensation of unease. Will I ever be such a happy bride? And then it is time to pick up her 20-foot long train. It takes us more than an hour to stuff her and her dress into the white limo.

Somehow we make it to the church on time.

It is not until later at the church that I spot BJ. He's standing at the back wearing a white shirt, a dove grey jacket, and black trousers. He doesn't smile and neither do I, but my breath catches. I quickly look away from his seductively dangerous eyes.

Sweet Jesus. I'm in love with the guy.

The wedding goes without a hitch. Of course, I don't catch the bridal bouquet even though Ella deliberately aims it in my direction. A woman I don't know lunges in front of me and catches it. She seems so excited, I can't even be annoyed with her.

Afterwards, when we are taking photographs, I manage to catch Jake.

'Where's Lily?' I ask him.

He tells me that she is observing the Chinese confinement tradition that doesn't allow her to leave the house for a whole month.

'Really?'

'Yes, really. She has to be on a special bland diet of soups and rice. And there is whole list of forbidden foods: raw fruit, vegetables, coffee, seafood, or anything cold.'

'Oh my God!'

'You think that's bad,' Jake says. 'Poor thing is not even allowed to bathe. All that's allowed is wipe-downs twice a week using washcloths steeped in smelly herbal medicine.'

'Well, she's made of sterner stuff than me then,' I say.

With a sigh Jake tells me that her grandmother, a woman that he describes as "formidable," is staying at the house overseeing to the torture. After the possessive kiss I saw Jake give Lily, I can only imagine how happy he will be once the 31 days are up.

'Can I speak to you later tonight at Ma's?' I ask casually.

'Is anything wrong?'

'Not really.'

He frowns. 'Do you want to talk about it now?'

'No, no, it can definitely wait.'

The reception is held in a large banquet room at the same venue. There are speeches and toasts. BJ is only a table away, but Jake is at the same table as me, so I dare not even look at him. Then the couple stands up to have their first dance. I turn my head towards the door and freeze.

Lupo is standing there.

He is browner than everybody else in the room and he is staring at me. I stand up as inconspicuously as possible and casually head towards him.

'What the hell are you doing here?' I whisper fiercely.

'I've come for you, Bella.'

'What?'

'I realize now what a big mistake I made, what a *stronzo* I have been, so I have come for you. I'm in love with you, Layla.'

My mouth drops open. And then I remember where I am. I grab his arm and drag him down the corridor. I open the first door we come across. It is a slightly smaller reception room with red carpets, rows of stacked chairs, and a musty smell.

I close the door, putting some distance between us, and look at his handsome face. I didn't notice it before, but he looks a lot like Enrique Iglesias. But what is really surprising is that I feel nothing. Not even rage. In fact, I am shocked that I ever thought he was worth climbing into bed with. Other than his looks, he has nothing. There is not even sexual attraction.

'How did you find me?'

He shrugs. 'I asked your mother, no?'

'You went to my ma's house?' I wail in dismay.

'Of course. Don't worry. I told her I was your friend.'

I breathe a sigh of relief. 'I'm sorry you've come all this way, but I'm not in love with you,' I say coldly. I need to get rid of him as soon as possible.

'No, you are just saying that because of what Gabriella told you. It's not true, you know. I was never in love with her.'

'I found someone else.'

'Who?' he demands angrily, his chest puffing up like a fighting cockerel's.

'Does it matter?'

'Yes, it matters. You are my girl. Who is this man?'

He takes a step forward and tries to put his arm around me. I pull away and he tightens his hold.

'Let go of me,' I say with gritted teeth.

'Don't be like that,' he cajoles and moves his face forward. I am just about to knee him in the balls when the door crashes open and BJ stands there, rigid with fury. His face is a thundercloud. His eyes are dangerously narrowed and cold, the whites laced with red. A muscle in his face twitches madly. I have never seen him in such a state. Not even in the pit.

He snarls more than speaks. 'Take your hand off her.'

Lupo shrivels before him. He looks like a man about to vomit. He looks at me and

back to BJ and the penny drops. He starts backing away with his hands raised in the air. 'I want no trouble,' he mumbles. What a coward.

When he is closer BJ leans forward slightly and, perfectly composed, utters, 'Don't ever come back.'

The door closes and we stare at each other. Then he walks towards me and pulls me into his solid muscles.

'What the fuck was my woman doing with that spineless little cunt?'

I look up at him. I can feel the aggression radiating off him. 'He's my ex.'

I twine my fingers in his hair, rising up on my tiptoes to gently place my lips on his. His hand snakes around my body and his mouth claims me. It is a demanding, aggressive, passionate kiss. I get so lost in it I don't even hear the door open until Jake's voice is upon us like the crack of a whip.

'What the fuck?'

I pull away from BJ's lips and still in his embrace, turn towards Jake. He is staring at me in disbelief. I feel the blood drain from my face. I open my mouth.

'Step away from him,' he says clearly, staring at BJ with murderous fury.

For a second I think about disobeying him, but I know that I need him on my side. I quickly squeeze BJ's hand and move aside.

'I can explain everyth—'

It goes down so fast, I don't actually see how it happens. One moment Jake is looming in the corridor, the next he is flying towards BJ. I am so shocked to see my brother attacking BJ, I can't even scream. For several seconds I stand and watch Jake swing his arm into BJ. I know BJ is not fighting back, just avoiding the blows. The first two hits don't catch. The third lands and BJ staggers back slightly and knocks a table. A glass vase full of fake flowers falls to the ground. Flowers go flying. The sight of it somehow galvanizes me.

'Stop it. Stop it,' I scream.

But neither man stops. I run towards them and both men look at me and growl for me to stay out.

'I'm pregnant,' I sob. 'I'm pregnant.'

For a shocked second everyone freezes.

Then all hell breaks loose.

TWENTY-FIVE

Layla

'**Y**ou fucking crazy son of a bitch. You didn't even use a fucking condom! That's my sister, you fucking dog,' Jake roars and swings out hard. BJ, still shell-shocked by my announcement, stumbles back against a pile of stacked chairs. The chairs go crashing and BJ falls over with them.

Both men are on the floor. Jake has BJ by the throat and he is choking him to death. Pure, uncontrollable panic surges through me. I run screaming towards them and drop to my knees beside them. 'Please, Jake,' I beg desperately, my hand uselessly trying to pull his away from BJ's throat. 'Please. Please don't. I love him,' I plead.

BJ swivels incredulous eyes towards me. Jake stiffens, but his hands are still frozen around BJ's throat.

I am sobbing hard now. 'He's the only one for me. If you love me please, please, I beg you, don't hurt him.'

Suddenly BJ chokes out, 'What're you going to do? Kill me? You can't fucking control everything in your world. I wanted to tell you, out of respect, man to man, but the fact is, your sister is all grown up and she wanted to tell you herself. But since you've ruined that possibility for her, here's how it's going down. I fucking love her, man. I've loved her since I was 14.'

I hold my face in the palms of my hands and stare incredulously at BJ. Jake sits back, his hands falling to his sides, his chest heaving. He stares at BJ coldly. 'If you cause her to shed one single tear, I swear, I'll make you cry blood. Then, I *will* fucking kill you.'

There is a trickle of crimson flowing from the side of BJ's mouth. He wipes it with the back of his hand. His shirtfront is smeared red.

'I won't,' he says clearly.

Jake gets to his feet, straightens himself, and sighs. He sounds defeated. He looks at me, and his eyes are sad. He wanted better for me. 'I'll see you at my home, later tonight?'

Unable to speak, I nod. Jake closes the door softly behind him and I run to BJ.

I touch the swelling on his jaw. 'Oh my God. It must hurt like hell.'

'Can't feel a thing. Too wired up.'

'I'm so sorry, BJ. This is the second time you've taken a hit for me.'

'Third time,' he corrects softly.

I frown. 'Third?'

'First time was when I fought Jake. He's a strong fighter, but I'm trained and he's not. I could have taken him, but I didn't.'

I remember that I had to look away at the ferocity with which he dispatched The Devil's Hammer. 'Why didn't you?'

'Why doesn't Batman kill the Joker?'

'I don't know. Why?'

'I wasn't being magnanimous or a hero when I drank a couple of cans of stout and allowed myself to fight loose and stupid. It was because of you. At the heart of my mercy was self-interest. I didn't want to vanquish Layla's brother and turn him into an unforgiving foe. Sometimes, your rival today becomes a vehicle for your legacy tomorrow. I wanted us to be equals. Sure I like Jake, but I've gone out of my way to maneuver myself into a place where he owes me one.'

Shocked by his confession, I sit back and stare at him. 'Were you really telling the truth when you told Jake that you love me?'

He expels the air in his chest in a rush. 'Love you? You're like a hundred flashbulbs in my face, Layla. You blind me. You always have. Ever since you trooped into church with your brothers, all of you wearing the old curtains my grandmother had donated to the charity shop. My mother sniggered, but my heart swelled just to look at you. Just to know that such beauty existed in this world. I tried to fight it. I even pretended to myself that you were a spoilt little brat. All these years.' He shook his head. 'Every conceivable type of woman. But none would ever do. My heart was taken."

I feel almost euphoric. 'So that's why you have the Layla tiepin.'

He flushes, the area above his cheekbones becoming dark red. 'Yeah I bought that when I was 15. One day, I promised myself, I'm going to walk down the aisle with that girl and I'm gonna wear it. But then you fell and when I went to help you up, you treated me as if I was a lump of dog shit. I realized you were too grand for me. So I killed the love in my heart. Or rather I thought I had, but I was just kidding myself.'

'I love you, BJ,' I whisper.

He swallows hard.

'It's not a death sentence,' I joke weakly.

He looks down. 'You don't understand. I thought you'd never say it. I thought …. You don't know how long I have waited to hear you say that,' he mutters close to my ear, his voice raspy and broken.

And suddenly I see the sweetness of this beautiful man. 'I love you so much I could die,' I say softly.

He lifts his head, his dark eyes shining. 'Say it again,' he commands.

'I love you so much I could die.'

'Again.'

This time the words roll out of me like a river breaking a dam.

He carefully wipes all expression off his face. 'Were you telling the truth? About the pregnancy? Or was it just to stop Jake from beating the shit out of me?' he asks lightly, but I know him well now. His whole body is tense.

I grin happily. 'Clearblue digital confirmed last night that we just contributed to the world's overpopulation problem.'

He stares at me with wide eyes. 'Fuck woman. Just for once can't you be like your brother's wife and give me a pair of baby shoes instead of this insensitive, sassy bullshit,' he croaks.

I look around the room, locate my purse a few feet away, and reach out for it. I take out a little box of baby shoes and shove it into his chest. 'There you go,' I cry triumphantly.

To my shock, tears fill his eyes.

I feel my eyes prickling too. 'Jesus, BJ. If I'd known it was that easy to make you cry I'd have got pregnant sooner.'

'I hate clichés, but fucking hell, Layla. This is the best day of my goddamn life.' He grins and I can feel the happiness pouring out of him. He stands suddenly, grabs my waist, and lifts me up as high as his arms can reach, whirling me round and round. I know he is doing it because I had told him about Lily's experience and how special I thought it was.

I start laughing. 'You're making me dizzy.'

'I know,' he laughs. 'That was the plan. You're always quiet when you're dizzy.'

'Why don't you use your usual way?' I tease.

He puts me down. 'I was saving that for last,' he says and covers my mouth with his own.

When he lifts his head, my insides are all gooey and melted. 'We're going to rule the world, aren't we?' I say dreamily.

He grins. 'Absolutely. I'll be the king and you'll be my queen.'

'And we'll sit on gold thrones.'

He touches my face. 'Oh Layla. You're the dream I didn't even dare have.'

I can't stop smiling. 'I've always wanted to be the dream someone didn't dare have.'

'I guess you'll have to marry me now, and in a hurry too, won't you?'

'Is that your idea of a proposal, BJ Pilkington?'

'No, I'll do a proper job, later, when I'm between your legs.'

'Oh my!'

'Come on. Let's get out of here.'

'Yes, lets,' I say drunk with love. Unable to believe where my day has ended. I was worried about telling Jake about BJ and telling BJ about the baby. And now everything has just fallen into place in the most extraordinary way. I know Jake *will* come around. BJ is happy about the baby. And everything is just so, so, so perfect.

TWENTY-SIX

Layla

It is 8:00 by the time I make it to Jake's house. All the lights are on and in one of the upstairs windows I can see the silhouette of Lily's grandmother cradling my niece in her arms. Anxiously, I go in through the kitchen hoping to meet my mother first. Shane is sitting with his legs up on a chair and eating a strawberry trifle.

'Hey, Bear,' he says, licking the spoon.

'Good you are in time for dinner,' Ma says, not looking up from chopping vegetables.

'How come he gets to eat dessert before dinner?' I ask.

'Because I'm not staying for dinner,' Shane says.

'Shane, I need to talk to Ma,' I tell him pointedly.

'Don't mind me,' he says, not moving from his chair.

My mother looks up. 'What do you want to tell your old mother? That you've got a man.'

I stare at her shocked. 'Yes, how did you know?'

'Do you think I'm stupid, Layla?'

'I'll be damned,' Shane says, grinning and slapping his thigh. 'Who's the poor sod?'

'Of course, I know,' my mother says. 'You've been walking around with your head in the clouds for at least a month now. So I checked with Queenie and she told me he is a good boy. One of ours. And I have been patiently waiting for you to tell me all about it. Sit down then.'

Bemused and pleasantly surprised at how easy all of this is turning out to be, I sit down and tell them that it's BJ.

'What? BJ!' Shane exclaims with a frown. 'Shit, Layla, he must be the worst man-whore in all of England and Scotland.'

'You're a fine one to talk,' I snap at my brother, glancing worriedly at my mother.

But my mother is not worried at all. 'Billy Joe is a good lad,' she defends. 'He'll be good to you. He's always had a soft spot for you.'

'You knew he had a soft spot for me?' I ask dazed.

'Of course. You could see it a mile off. He used to stare so intently at you in church I thought his eyes would pop out.'

I grin. The way my mother exaggerates anyone would think I was some great beauty. 'Really?'

'Him and half the boys in the congregation,' Shane adds.

'Yes, poor Jake always had his hands full giving them all dirty looks,' my mother says.

'So you think I made a good choice?' I ask my mother happily.

'I fucking don't,' Shane says.

But Ma is unshakeable in her convictions. 'I do. But it's Jake you'll have to convince. He's in the library. Go on and talk to him before dinner.'

'Uh, Ma. I've got something else to tell you.'

She stops chopping. Her mouth drops open. 'Oh, Layla. You're not.'

I bite my lip. 'I am.'

'What?' Shane asks looking from me to Ma and back to me with confusion. 'You're what?'

'I'm pregnant.'

Shane's eyes widen. 'Poor BJ!'

'Come here,' my mother says. From her face I can tell she is fighting hard to keep from crying.

I go and crouch next to her. Up close, I see all the fine lines that fan out from her eyes. My mother is getting old. The idea is distressing. I don't want my mother to grow old. I don't ever want to lose her. She holds my face between her work-worn palms and kisses my forehead. 'My mother was right. It is never the wild ones that get knocked up. It's always the good girls. How far along are you?'

'Just about four weeks.'

She nods.

'I'm sorry, Ma.'

She takes her hands away from my face. 'Don't be sorry. He's a good boy. He'll do right by you. Now go and talk to your brother.'

I grasp my mother's hands and kiss them. 'I love you, Ma.'

'I love you too, Layla,' she says and tears glimmer in her eyes.

On my way out, I punch Shane hard on the shoulder.

'Did you see what she did?' I hear him ask.

I don't hear her reply. I walk along the corridor and knock nervously on my brother's door.

'Come in, Layla,' Jake says.

Taking a deep breath, I enter. My brother is sitting behind his desk. He leans back in his chair and looks at me expressionlessly.

'Look, first of all I want to say I'm really sorry that I didn't tell you sooner, but you were so excited and happy about Lilliana's arrival that I just didn't want to spoil it.'

My brother nods. 'So you're in love with him.'

'Yes. Very much.'

He sighs. 'I wanted better for you.'

'I know you did, but BJ is my destiny, like Lily is yours.'

'I know. But all said and done, he's in the drug trade, Layla. He'll make a mistake one day and he'll go to prison. Are you prepared for that?'

'No.'

'Then use that great love he has for you to make him give it up. It's not like he needs to do it. He already has more money than he knows what to do with. He's got his clubs and pubs and all his properties.'

I move deeper into the room. Jake is right. BJ is going to be a dad. He doesn't need to be involved in the drug business.

'Now is your best opportunity, Layla. Before you get married. Lay down your terms. You'll be a mother soon. Think of your children.'

'OK, I will.'

'I want you to be happy. You know that, don't you?'

I walk around the chair and touch his cheek. 'I know that. I didn't want to disobey you. It just happened.'

He smiles sadly. 'Just remember, no matter what happens, I am always here for you.'

'Thank you.'

'How many weeks gone are you?'

'Four.'

'Are you happy?'

'It's all so perfect I couldn't have planned it better.'

He grins. 'I'm proud of you, Layla.'

I grin back. 'Can you believe it? I'm gonna be somebody's mummy.'

'You'll be a good mother, Layla. I can feel it in my bones.'

-All of me loves all of you-

TWENTY-SEVEN

Layla

Ki shan i Romani - Adoi san' i chov'hani.
Wherever gypsies go - there the witches are,
we know.

I clasp my hands together and fix my gaze
on his face. 'BJ, what will happen to me and
our baby if something happens to you? Like
you get caught by the police.'

'I won't get caught. I told you nothing passes through my hands.'

'There's no such thing as never. There are always people who will betray you to save their own skin or mistakes or an envious friend.'

His face closes over. 'What do you want me to say, Layla?'

'I want you to give it up. I want you to give it up, because if you don't, I will never, ever feel secure.'

'It's what I am, Layla.'

'No, it's not what you are. It's what you do.'

He covers his face with his hands, rubbing them upwards towards his head. 'What if I say I can't stop? Will you leave me?'

I drop my head, because I don't want him to see how crushed and disappointed I am. If he had asked for something that was important to him, I would have moved heaven and earth to give it to him. It means all his words are empty and meaningless. He doesn't truly love me. Not the way I do.

'Well?' he prompts.

I clear my face of the pain I am feeling and look up. 'No,' I say dully. 'I won't leave you.'

'What if I said that I've already taken steps to get out of that business?'

I hardly dare believe it. 'You have?'

He nods. 'Don't you know? I'd do anything for you. Anything.'

The joy I feel is what I imagine being hit by very mild lightning must be like. I feel my skin tingle and my entire body wants to shake, jump, and dance around. 'You can't imagine how crushed and sad I was when you said you couldn't do it.'

'Good,' he says and laughs, and I decide that now is the best time to give a little of my bad news.

'By the way,' I say as casually as I can, 'Jake wants us to have a commitment ceremony.'

'A fucking what?'

I nod, trying to keep the amusement from my face. 'You heard correctly.'

'You better be kidding me ...'

I shake my head slowly, not daring to say another word, laughter bubbling inside me.

'The paranoid motherfucker.'

The laugher spews forth.

'You're enjoying this aren't you?' he accuses.

'I have to drink the brew too, you know.'

'So what are you laughing about, then?'

'If you could see your face.'

'When does he want this ceremony to take place?'

'Tomorrow night. It's a full moon. Good for spells.'

'Oh for fuck's sake. I don't believe this shit. Did he have one with Lily?'

'That's exactly what I asked him.'

'And what did he say?'

'He said Lily isn't his sister, but if she was he would have insisted on it.'

He shakes his head in wonder. 'Let me see if I've got this right. We sit inside a circle at some outdoor location and make promises to each other in front of some shaman.'

'And drink a potion.'

His eyes narrow suspiciously. 'Exactly what's in the brew?'

I chew my lower lip. 'I think articles of our used clothing, animal lung of some sort, definitely liver, fat, and probably salt. It's usually put into love charms to ensure the duration of the attachment.'

He folds his arms. 'All right. If it makes you happy and you're OK with it, then I am too.'

I laugh. 'Actually, Jake says since I am pregnant I only need to have a very small sip. A taste were his exact words. You'll have to drink most of it.'

'I knew it,' he bursts out. 'This is to punish me, isn't it?'

I'm dying to laugh. 'A bit.'

'Other men get a stag night with booze and strippers from their brother-in-law-to-be and I get this!'

'We can get some strippers for the ceremony if you want.'

'You find this all very funny, don't you, Miss Eden?'

And I can no longer hold back the laughter. Eventually he laughs too. When we

stop, he looks into my eyes and his voice is very serious. 'Jake knows nothing. I'd walk over hot coals for you. Drinking fat, liver, and lung, I could do it every day for the rest of my life if it means having you.'

'I love you, BJ Pilkington. I really, really do.'

'By the way, can they make that article of clothing one of your used panties? It might make the lung, liver, and fat a bit more palatable.'

'Oh, you disgusting man, Mr. Pilkington,' I scold, but I am laughing and so crazy in love with him, I could pop him between two slices of bread and eat him for lunch.

Despite the fact that Jake glowers all through the commitment ceremony, it turns out to be something different and more precious than I imagined it to be. One day I will tell my grandchildren about it. BJ's mother gives me an antique shawl. My mother gives me a gold chain with a sapphire pendant.

It's a cold night and we all dress in warm clothing. The moon is very bright, hanging like a lantern in the sky as we drive out to a wooded area and walk to a clearing.

The shaman is already waiting for us.

God only knows where Jake found her. She is an ancient creature, straight out of the witches' scene in Macbeth. Hunched underneath an old, black cloak, her face in the moonlight is craggy with deep grooves and her skin is mottled with coffee-colored spots. Her hair is silvery and surprisingly thick. One eye is completely white, the pupil covered over with cataract, and the other is jet-black and alive with an animal-like alertness. She wears a red rose tucked behind her ear.

Her body is thin and pitiful, but her movements are as stubborn and headstrong as that of a wild boar. When she extends a withered hand from the inky folds of her cloak, I see that every one of her bony fingers is heavy with an assortment of large and intricate rings. There are ancient symbols carved into the stones.

She tells BJ and me to take off our shoes, pull our prayer shawls over our heads, and sit cross-legged inside the circle that she draws with a chalky stone. Then she half-squats on a low, four-legged stool and surrounds herself with the tools of her trade. Feathers, a fan, shells, and red and black candles, which she lights and shades with glass coverings. She unrolls a long ribbon and ties an end to both our wrists.

'Are you ready?' she croaks.

We nod.

She starts by inviting and welcoming helping spirits and the spirits of deceased

 208

loved ones. She looks at me directly. There is something enchanted and mysterious about her dark, bottomless eye. Her mystique is bewitching. I have the impression that I am staring into the eye of an ancient mystic feline. Timeless and weightless. That my spirit has intertwined with hers in an invisible sublime dance.

'Think of them, all the ones who have left you and they will come.'

I think of Father and call him to come.

Her black eye fixes on me again. 'It is always as forecast and necessary,' she says intriguingly.

Then she begins to sing in a language I do not understand, plaintively, as if she is calling to a lost love. Her voice echoes through the night. Afterwards, she burns some sweet herbs and offers rice to the spirits who have come to witness the ceremony.

BJ and I exchange bracelets made of twine with each other. Afterwards, we make our vows of fidelity and loyalty to each other. First to go is BJ. By the light of the candles, he recites the vows we have both chosen to make.

'I, Billy Joe Pilkington, by the life that courses within my blood and the love that resides within my heart, take thee Layla Eden to my hand, my heart, and my spirit to be my chosen one. To desire thee and be desired by thee. To possess thee and be possessed by thee without sin or shame, for naught can exist in the purity of my love for thee. I promise to love thee wholly and completely without restraint, in sickness and in health, in plenty and in poverty, in life and beyond, where we shall meet, remember, and love again. I shall not seek to change thee in any way. I shall respect thee, thy beliefs, thy people, and thy ways as I respect myself.'

Staring into his eyes, I repeat the same vow and it feels as if my heart will burst with the love I have for him.

Then it is time to drink the thick brown brew. It is truly disgusting. Even the tiny little sip I consume coats my tongue and makes me feel downright queasy. BJ is the real hero of the piece though. He drinks it all without fuss.

Later he whispers in my ear. 'I'm gonna need to forget this taste. Get ready to have your pussy in my mouth for a very long time.'

I try to suppress the giggles, but I am not very successful. I feel a great wave of love wash over me for this wonderful man.

'Jeez, Layla, don't look at me like that unless you want me to drag you behind some bushes and rape you.'

'Do you ever wonder what would have happened if I hadn't gone into your bedroom and tried to take your tiepin?'

He shudders. 'No.'

TWENTY-EIGHT

Layla

After the ceremony my life becomes a whirl of frantic activity. There are so many things to decide: locations, bridesmaid dresses, shoes, music, caterers, invitations, photographer, the cake, videographer, invitations, stationery, rings, favors, transportation, and, of course, my dress. BJ hires a wedding planner. She is so brilliant that I can't even imagine doing it without her. It's a great comfort to simply call her if

I have a query or worry and know that she is already on top of it.

My mother makes an appointment with Thelma Madine, the dress designer. Thelma Madine is exactly how she is on TV. Warm, talented, and a practical businesswoman to the core. She would have made a good gypsy.

'How big do you want your dress to be?' she asks.

'Big,' my mother says. 'She's my only girl. My Princess.'

'Oh, Ma,' I say. 'It's a shotgun wedding. I was thinking of a simple mermaid dress.'

'Simple!' my mother explodes. 'Where's the fun in that?' She throws her hands up animatedly. 'This is a once-in-a-lifetime event. Who are you to deny yourself the best and most beautiful wedding dress possible on your big day?'

My mother is right. A wedding should be fun. Every gypsy wedding that I have attended, even the tackiest, most over-the-top ones with white stretch-limos and chocolate fountains have been far more enjoyable, exciting, and dramatic than any of the elegant, color-coordinated, chair-covered, non-gypsy ones. And when I think back, a sedate wedding is classy and admirable, but it is the big gypsy weddings that are unforgettable.

I look at Thelma. 'You know what, I will have that big ball gown after all.'

But Thelma is not the queen of the gypsy bridal dress for nothing. 'I can do you a mermaid wedding dress and make your mother happy too,' she declares confidently.

'Really?'

'Yes, really.'

And she is as good as her word. The very next day she comes back with two sketches. Ma and me agree on a fit-and-flare design with a sweetheart neckline, pearls on the bodice, and hundreds and hundreds of taffeta handkerchiefs sewn together to make the billowing skirt and train. It comes with a little bolero for the church. The whole ensemble is in shades of oyster.

In a week Thelma calls me for my first fitting. The three of us drive over to her shop. It is exciting and frightening. I'm not sure if she can really pull of a big mermaid dress.

'Come in,' she says. I can tell she is eager to show us her creation. She takes us quickly to the back of the shop. In a move that is pure drama, she pauses in front of a closed door, and with her hand on the handle, turns to us and asks, 'Are you ready for this?'

My mother, Maddy, and I nod. While butterflies flutter in my stomach, she theatrically flings open the door.

The dress is on a stand, its train of thousands of taffeta squares spread out like an enormous fish tail behind it. I gasp and stare in amazement. My mother squeals like a young girl and Maddy claps her hands with delight. Any fears I had that it would be tacky or too My Big Fat Gypsy Wedding are laid to rest forever. The dress is amazing. Totally and utterly spectacular. It is a masterpiece, pure and simple.

The days pass in a blur of hectic activity and excitement. Only moments shine through with full HD clarity. Those rare moments I look at in amazed wonder, sometimes disbelief. So this is my life. A week before the wedding, I give up my apartment, transport most of my stuff into BJ's home, and move into my mother's house. At this point BJ and I are no longer able to see each other alone and the separation is pure torture.

But suddenly, before I know it, my wedding day is upon me. I wake up early, a bundle of nerves, and lie very quietly in the dark. Already, I can hear my mother and aunts moving about the house. I put my hand on my stomach. It's still flat, but my baby is growing inside.

'We're getting married today,' I whisper, and a thrill of excitement runs through me.

Maddy is the first to arrive and we eat breakfast in my bedroom together. We speak in whispers and giggle quietly as if we are children on a midnight adventure.

The hairdresser arrives at seven. Ma makes her a cup of coffee and she sets about separating my hair into two parts, gathering the top half into a bun at the back of my head and putting corkscrew curls into the lower half and leaving them trailing down my back and shoulders. She fits a princess tiara over my head, and the make-up artist takes me on. She spends an hour on my face, painting, dabbing, drawing, brushing, and then gluing on individual spikes of false eyelashes.

By now the house is crowded with friends and relatives bringing presents. Gypsies are generous gift givers and the pile of presents soon fills the dining table and spills onto the floor, and still more well-wishers are flooding through the doors. Ma breaks into the stack of champagne cases and the house heaves as if it is a party.

Then the dress arrives.

From my window I watch Thelma and her two assistants carefully carry it into the house. They bring it upstairs to my room and Thelma and her assistants help me into it. My heart is racing with nerves.

'Oh, oh, oh,' exclaims a delighted Maddie. 'You look stunning.'

When I have been laced into the dress and the veil fixed into place, I walk over to the mirror with bated breath.

And ... almost do not recognize the person in the mirror. I look like I have stepped out of a page of a fairytale. Ma, who has changed into a pretty grey-blue dress, has tears in her eyes. She dabs them away carefully with the edge of a tissue.

'You look absolutely beautiful, Layla,' she says.

'You were right, Ma. The dress is perfect.'

My mother smiles through her tears.

Thelma and her assistants pick up the train and hem of the skirt as I go through the door, preventing me from stepping on it and falling headlong down the stairs. They carry the train as I go down the stairs in my pearl-encrusted slippers.

And then I am standing in front of Jake. He looks gorgeous in his grey morning suit. His eyes are so bright and full of pride.

'Oh! Layla. If only Da could see you. You're the princess he always said you were,' he says.

Lily smiles. The confinement thing has really worked. She is glowing and beautiful. 'I always knew he would get you.'

'You did?'

She nods. 'He's a good guy. I'll never forget what he did for Jake and me. I'm so happy for you. Be happy always, Layla.'

Then Dominic and Shane come to kiss me. They look incredibly handsome in their new suits. Dominic nods approvingly, and even Shane forgets to be a smartass. 'You look truly beautiful,' he says sincerely.

As I walk to the front door, everybody takes pictures and videos.

Gingerly, I step out of my mother's house and scream. I can't believe it. I don't know whether it is Jake or BJ who has arranged it, but it is the last thing I am expecting. A glass carriage is waiting on the road. It is dainty and ornate and quite simply magical, something you would see in a Disney movie. It has two grooms in livery and two white steeds with plumed headdresses.

'BJ insisted on it,' Jake says.

Jake gets in first and then Thelma helps me into the carriage so that I am sitting opposite him and my train is coiled between us. The door closes and we are off, with passing cars tooting their horns at us all the way to the church. Complete strangers hang their heads out of their cars, smile, wave, and wish me well.

By the time we get to the church, we are 30 minutes late and the bridesmaids and flower girls are all lined up and waiting. Maddy winks at me. Jake reaches over and squeezes my hand.

'Thank you, Jake. Thank you for everything,' I say. My voice sounds shaky.

'Never mind that. Don't ruin your mascara,' he says, his voice is gruff.

Thelma and her assistants help me out of the carriage. I step out into the sunshine. It is a beautiful, still spring day. There are strangers gathered all around watching the wedding procession. And suddenly I have an attack of nerves. I turn blindly to Jake. I've been doing that since I was child. Always Jake. Fighting all my battles.

'I'm with you every step of the way,' he says, holding his hand out.

I take it, and just like that I am no longer nervous that I will trip, fall, or make a mistake. I am excited by the future that awaits me in the church. We walk up the steps to the church, my fingers resting lightly on his forearm. The sound of the wedding march floats out the double doors.

We make our way to the entrance, instantly I see my bridegroom. All in white. So broad and tall and wonderful. In the periphery of my vision I can see my mother, my brothers, my friends, acquaintances, and even strangers lining the back pews. In a flash of white, BJ turns and everyone else disappears. Our eyes meet and we're alone in the church. Only him and me.

'Wow,' he mouths silently, his eyes blazing possessively.

Then my brother is moving forward and my legs follow his lead. I can feel the heavy train trailing for yards behind me, hear the swishing of the taffeta, smell the sweet perfume of the bouquets, and sense the solid muscles of my brother's arm under my hand, but I am in a total daze. My eyes never leave BJ.

My brother takes his arm away and I look at him stupidly. He smiles and I turn my face back to BJ. He puts out a hand and gently pulls me towards him. He is so big and beautiful, I cannot believe that he is really mine. The tiepin that had started

everything glints on his cravat, catching my eye. It doesn't match and yet is perfect.

The vicar begins to recite our vows and I follow, repeating every word carefully, in awe of the sounds that leave my lips. For they come directly from some deep, unknown place inside my being.

'I do,' I say.

BJ slips the ring onto my finger and the vicar pronounces us man and wife. He doesn't have time to give BJ permission to kiss the bride. BJ has already leaned over the yards and yards of material separating us and found my mouth. The congregation erupts: cheering, clapping, and whistling. We are a rowdy bunch, us gypsies.

Thelma leads me to a small room at the side of the church. Carefully, she removes the veil and the bolero. The hairdresser touches up my hair and they help me out of the door. I stand for a moment at the entrance of the church. Then I see a brilliant flash of white and the crowds part to let him through. BJ stops in front of me and stares transfixed, his eyes devouring me. The dress has been laced up too tight to take a deep calming breath so I take quick shallow breaths through my mouth. He takes my hand.

'You ordered one princess?' I whisper.

'I did. And you ordered one love-sick husband?'

'Husband,' I repeat. The word lands onto my tongue as light as a butterfly. I find it to be a familiar word that brings peace to my entire body. As if I was always meant to be Mrs. Billy Joe Pilkington.

TWENTY-NINE

Layla

After my ultimate wish-upon-a-star, fairytale wedding, BJ whisks me off to Tuscany for our honeymoon. We stay in a magnificent palazzo near Maremma's woodlands. For four passion-drenched, slothful days we do nothing but explore each other. Once we wake up at dawn we ride into the outstandingly beautiful and wild countryside.

BJ is a strong rider, but so am I and it is exhilarating. When we stop we are both flushed and aroused. In the clear fresh morning air, we tear each other's clothes off and indulge in the delight of outdoor sex. At the end of it, I'm startled by an audience. A pair of beautiful roe deer wearing their reddish summer coats are looking at us curiously. We freeze, BJ still deep inside me, and stay still until they amble away.

'Wasn't that beautiful?' I whisper.

'Everything with you is,' he says.

Everyday we discover new things about each other. I now know that BJ doesn't have breakfast. He has eight raw eggs blended with a banana and some milk. And he knows that I like a selection of warm pastries from the village woman. And that I'll quite happily drink chilled, raw goat's milk with them.

In the afternoon, when it is too hot to do anything, we swim lazily consuming countless ice lollies by the pool. At night, we eat thin-crust pizza cooked in a traditional wood oven, or even barbeque fish we bought from the outdoor market on the terrace. Once BJ makes us a pasta pomodoro with steak. I discover he's not a bad cook.

'Did your mother teach you?' I ask.

'No, it's Bertie's recipe.'

Tonight, he's taking me to a famous restaurant a few miles away. The man who cleans the pool tells us that one has not lived until you've tried Il Cinghiale Nero's

signature dish of wild boar and porcini mushrooms.

I soak in the bath inside the high-ceilinged, pink marble bathroom until he scoops me out and carries me, still dripping with soapsuds, to our enormous bedroom. He throws me on the bed and dives in after me. He has his own way of drying me. It doesn't involve a towel, but it does feature a great deal of effort on his part, and wet sheets. Afterwards, as I lay on my back satiated, he grasps my ankle in his hand and brings it to his mouth.

'It's amazing how brown you have become in four days.'

I look into his love-drunk eyes. 'Wait until you see me at the end of the week.'

He leans back on the pillows, eyes half-mast, and watches me slip into a sultry, red knee-length dress with a daring décolleté. I slip on exotic, toe-ring sandals with straps embellished with turquoise stones. I brush my hair, apply mascara and lip-gloss, and dab perfume on to my pulse points.

'Come here,' he says.

I cross my arms across my chest. 'Nope, I'm not having you ruin my primping. You can have me after you feed me.'

He bounds up suddenly, sending me screaming out of the bedroom and through the tall corridor with its gilded panels and oil paintings, then down the grand marble staircase. I stand at the foot of the stairs looking up, laughing and gasping for breath, and ready to bolt outside if he decides to come down after me, but he stands leaning on the banister.

'There'll be hell to pay if you keep it for later,' he calls out.

'Is that a threat?'

He grins. 'Consider it an invitation.'

I grin back. 'In that case, I accept.'

He nods and disappears back down the corridor.

The pool cleaner is right. It has to be the one of the best meals I've eaten in my life. It's when we're ordering dessert that our trouble starts.

I turn to BJ after ordering my sweet from the waiter, and he is scowling at me.

'What?' I ask.

'Stop fucking flirting with that waiter, or he'll find his pepper mill sticking out of his fucking ass.'

'Are you kidding me?'

'Does it look like I am?'

'I wasn't flirting.'

'No?'

'No,' I say very empathically.

'So what the hell was all that hair flicking and the "*si, si, sei troppo gentile*" all about, then?' he asks changing his voice to a mocking falsetto to imitate mine.

'That was me being polite,' I say, getting a bit irritated myself.

'How would you like it if I did that with the waitress?'

'I wouldn't mind at all. Go ahead. Be my guest,' I tell him.

A look crosses his face. 'All right. Just remember you started this.'

He looks around and catches the eye of the most attractive waitress in the restaurant and lifts his eyebrow. When she comes to him he gives her a slow smile and asks if she could bring a bottle of their best champagne.

She trots off and he smiles pleasantly at me. I am determined not to react so I smile back.

When she returns, totally ignoring me, he blatantly begins to flirt and laugh with her, blatantly. My blood begins to boil. Yes, it's true I did flirt with the waiter, but only lightly. He, on the other hand, was almost stripping her naked with his eyes.

At first I try my best not to show how furious I am. I tell myself that he's doing it deliberately. It's not like he truly wants her. He's just punishing me. I briefly toy with the idea of calling the waiter back and flirting in exactly the same way with him. See who cracks first. But I don't actually want to seriously flirt with another man on my honeymoon.

I could have held on and sat it out with my frozen smile if the quick-eyed slut had not given me a look that was at once pitying and triumphant. A look that said, *hey, you're a fool. Can't you see what your man is doing? How totally into me he is?*

Humiliated, I stand up. I don't have the car keys. Not that it matters. I wouldn't dare drive the powerful Maserati he has rented, especially on unfamiliar roads. Fuck him, I would rather walk the five miles back to the palazzo than stay here another second. Both of them turn to look at me. She seems glad that I might be leaving.

'Going somewhere, babe?' BJ asks sweetly.

'Nowhere that concerns you,' I answer with equal sweetness, and walk out of the restaurant.

Outside, I pause for a moment at the entrance. I am so angry I want to scream. How dare he behave like that on our honeymoon. I start walking fast in the direction we had come from. Fortunately, I am wearing flat sandals. I must have gone 20 yards before I hear the Maserati's engine idling along beside me.

'Need a lift somewhere?'

'What? Not taking your tart back with you?' I say huffily.

'Well, well, look who's all jealous?' His voice is rich with laughter.

His mirth irritates me. 'There is a difference between what I was doing and what you were engaging in! I was being polite and you were fucking her with your eyes.'

He laughs. His laughter is like smoke and silk. 'It'll take us forever to reach the palazzo at this rate.'

Even though the forecast called for a thunderstorm tonight, I am not prepared for the downpour that begins with large drops of hot rain that smells of dust. A couple fall on my head.

'Get in, Layla,' BJ says, his voice silky.

This time I open the door and get in, but I am determined to make him suffer for the humiliation he caused at the restaurant. I am going to give him the silent treatment.

THIRTY

BJ

I steal a sidelong glance at her. She was cute in the restaurant when she was acting all unconcerned while she was burning up with fury inside, but now that she is radiating waves of don't-touch-me she's smoking hot. It reminds me of what she used to be like. Having it inside this car with the smell of the thunderstorm raging outside, it's as sexy as hell.

I need to fuck my new wife.

Through the lashing rain I suddenly see it coming up ahead, a forest. This is it, real freedom, a centuries' old, living, breathing, magical wonderment. *Sometimes we need to let go of life's shackles and find oneness with nature.* Feeling reckless, my dick steering the vehicle, I veer off the motorway and head down a winding country lane. I don't need to look at Layla to know she is staring at me with narrowed eyes.

'Why the hell have you left the motorway?' she asks with a scowl.

'There's something I've always wanted to do,' I reply.

She stares at the rain lashing down on the windshield, the continuous streak left by the wipers. 'Well, whatever it is, count me out. I'm not going out in that rain.' she says in her best Ice Queen tone.

Excitement surges through my veins. I say nothing. Just stop the car, then make my way around to Layla's window.

I stand outside for moment, eyes focused on her. The gesticulation of her hands and exaggerated facial expression clearly indicate that she thinks I'm a raving fucking lunatic.

'It's bloody pouring,' she shouts, her voice barely audible.

I swipe at the water streaming down my face. Yeah, *like I hadn't fucking noticed.*

'If you don't get out now, I'll drag you the fuck out."

Her mouth drops open. A look flares through her eyes. I know that look too well.

She's going to fucking lock me out. Before she has time to react, my hand is on the handle and the door is open. I grab her and haul her out while she struggles like a wildcat.

'What the fuck has gotten into you?' she yells in my face.

Her fury is pure bliss against the backdrop of the thunderstorm. It makes my blood sing for her. I let go of her.

And she takes a step back. I watch the rain drench her, her dress becomes transparent. She's not wearing a bra. Her chest is heaving. Her nipples are as hard as stone. God! My wife is so beautiful. Sometimes I can't believe she is mine. My cock starts straining for release as if it is a loaded missile zeroing in on its target.

Her mouth drops open as it dawns on her exactly what's on my mind. 'If you think I'm going to have sex out here in the middle of nowhere after the stunt you pulled in the restaurant as well, you better think again.'

I start to laugh.

'What's so bloody funny?'

'You babe.'

'You have a sick sense of humor. Letting your pregnant wife freeze to death in the rain,' she shouts.

'You're not freezing. On a hot steamy night like this, rain is lovely.' I grab her arms and pull her body tight against me. 'We,' I growl in her ear, 'are going to fuck like we've never fucked before.'

'You HAVE got to be kidding!' Rain splatters onto her face and flows in her gorgeous mouth.

'I don't kid around about how, when, and where I fuck my wife.'

'I'm not rolling around in the mud while an avalanche of rain is being dumped on me from the heavens,' she snaps.

'Why the hell not? What could be more perfect? There's no one around for miles. It's hot and steamy. The rain beating down on us will be kinda sexy.'

'Quite frankly, because you don't bloody deserve it. How dare you flirt like that in front of me? I was humiliated,' she spits at me furiously.

'Next time remember that before you start giving other men the come-on.'

'Oh!' She stamps her foot in frustration. 'I was not giving him the come-on.'

'Well, in future bear in mind that we have different ideas about what equates to a come-on.'

'So you're not going to apologize?'

'What do you think?'

'I think you should.'

'I think we should have sex.'

'What about our clothes? How will we get them dried? How will we drive back in this condition?'

I grin. 'We'll turn up the temperature in the car and drive home nude,' I tell her.

'Oh BJ, this is really crazy.'

'No, this is exactly what we need.'

Layla raises her eyebrows disdainfully, but she's not fooling me. Her true resistance is actually gone. She, too, wants to have her hormone-loaded little pussy filled in the rainstorm. 'I've always imagined what it might be like to have wild, animalistic, outdoor sex in a steamy climate. OK, maybe it was without the rain, but right now, that just adds to the fantasy.'

There is a burst of thunder and it startles her. She jumps against me. I take that moment to grab her hand and pull her to the front of the car.

In the glare of the headlights she looks even more fuckable.

Her long hair is plastered to her body, and the outline of her hardened nipples, aching to be free from that dress, is even more pronounced. Naked, spread-eagle, and trapped under me is how I want her.

I move closer to press my rock hard cock into her pubic bone and pull her hair backwards, until she is arched across the hood. For a second I simply stop and look at her, spread out, the rain exploding like liquid bullets on her body. Mist, the steam rising from the hood of the car, surrounds us.

She is a work of art.

Leaning over my Princess, I run a hungry tongue along her slender neck, tracing the stretched muscles. She tilts her head back even further, and looking up at the sky, exhales deeply. Just like that I know she's ready. It's surrender, pure and simple.

I use my knees to spread her legs, then trace my hand up the inside of her leg under her dress and rip off her panties in a single action. The tearing sound mingles with the drumming of the rain on the hood of the car. Her body clenches in anticipation. I get a good feel of her pussy quivering and sweet with honey.

Using both my hands I tear her dress open and expose the firm, tanned flesh underneath. For a moment I lift my bulk backwards and delight in the sight of her magnificence, her naked breasts glistening in the rain and her pale stomach just beginning to swell writhing against mine. I place my lips against hers, undo my jeans and yank the clinging material away. Her rain-soaked mouth is sugar. *Ah! Layla. Layla. Layla. It was always only you.*

How could you be jealous of any other woman?

I move my mouth down to her right nipple, flicking and teasing while I roll the left nipple between my fingers squeezing intermittently. Ever since she became pregnant her nipples have become even more sensitive. The slightest touch is enough to get her going. She groans helplessly while I suck and run the edge of my teeth and tongue across the hard buds. I let my fingers play with the inviting softness of her slickly swollen pussy. She responds by involuntarily raising her head and chest.

I push her downwards to the metal again, spread her thighs wider and put my left arm under her shoulders so I can control her body. I insert two fingers into her honeyed pussy.

'Yes,' she moans.

But I don't give her what she wants. She wants speed, thickness. I deny her both. I keep my fingers moving slowly and using my thumb work her clit, feeling the frustration mounting in her body.

She thrusts her pubic area restlessly towards my hand.

Just as she's about to climax, I stop and withdraw my fingers from her begging pussy. Rearing back, I swipe the water from my eyes and wrap my mouth around one of her erect nipples. Sucking hard, I plunge my throbbing cock into her depths.

'Oh. My. God. BJ!'' she screams, her body arching like a pulled bow.

I swoop down on her other nipple and bite it. She screams again. I lift my head and watch the rain flow over the bitten nipple. I move closer and her whole body tenses as I trail my tongue on the other nipple. She trembles with anticipation.

She raises her head and looks at me, water running down her slack features.

'Were you flirting with that waiter?'

'No.' She swallows.

I slide my hands along her wet thighs.

 234

'Are you sure?'

She nods.

'Don't lie to me, Layla. We can't move from here until you tell me the truth.'

She licks her lips. 'All right. Yes, I did it to make you jealous.'

I squeeze her thighs and ram my blood-filled dick deep into her.

'Ahh...'

'You like that?'

'Yes.'

'Do you know what is going to happen to you if you do that again?'

She shakes her head.

'I'm going to fuck you for days. I will fill your belly with my cum and have it running out of every orifice. Do you understand?'

She nods.

'I didn't hear you.'

'Yes. I understand,' she mutters.

'Good,' I say and bite her other nipple. Her mouth opens in a scream and I cover it with mine. I plunge my tongue into her warmth, hook her tongue into my mouth, and suck it hard as I thrust into her.

I feel her pulse change and her muscles tighten around the base of my shaft. I release her tongue. She digs her fingers into my ass cheeks as the erratic spasms of pleasure erupt deep within her body.

'Oh God,' she cries, 'I'm coming.'

I feel her nails embed themselves into my ass, but I don't give a fuck. I'm oblivious to any pain as I hear her cry out in ecstasy as her orgasm rips through her body.

My cock pulsates and throbs and I drive to the hilt one last time. With a jerk I start filling her pretty little pink pussy with my hot cum. Wrapping her legs tightly around my waist she milks my body expertly.

-You are the color of my blood-

THIRTY-ONE

Layla

My mother says I must have been born under a lucky star: I've not experienced any morning sickness. I wanted to carry on working until the baby was due, but neither my family or BJ will stand for it. *What's the point if you are planning on giving it up after the baby is born anyway?* I suppose they have a point. Still, I would have preferred it to be my decision.

I stand in the shower, water sluicing down my shoulders onto my braided hair and dripping over my growing belly. In the fast-moving water, my growing mound looks like an eyeball. I imagine his tiny transparent fingers clutching and unclutching at nothing. An animal instinct makes me curve my hands around my belly protectively.

It is a constant source of wonder for me, knowing that a human being resides inside me. I think of his tiny little heart beating, his mouth opening and gulping amniotic fluid. During the ultrasound, it showed as a black bubble in his stomach. But the miracle that makes me smile the most is the thought that every half an hour or so his tiny bladder is emptying. My rude son is peeing inside me!

I wonder what he will smell like, how his story will unfold.

BJ wants to call him Tommy. Over my dead body, I informed him in no uncertain terms. I want my boy to be called Oliver or one of those really cool American cowboy names like Sundance or Texas Jack. At the very least, something proper like Charles or Phillip.

But Tommy is a proper Irish name, BJ insisted.

I love my husband to death, but Tommy? Ugh. No. Never. Like I said, over my dead body. I get out of the shower and rub rich coca butter on my tummy and hips

before I get dressed. BJ is in the gym. A one-hour loop of Lost Frequencies *Are You With Me* is playing in the background. I listen to it so often I am sure my son will be born humming this tune.

The phone rings. It's the hospital.

'Mrs. Pilkington?'

'Yes.'

'This is St. James Hospital. This is Nurse Mary Varenne."

'Hello.'

'Dr. Freedman would like to see you and your husband as soon as possible.'

Alarm bells start ringing in my head. I clutch the receiver with both hands. 'Why?' My voice is a frightened whisper.

'I'm afraid I'm not at liberty to say. But it is urgent that both your husband and you attend his surgery immediately.'

'What's wrong with my baby?'

'I'm sorry, Mrs. Pilkington, but I am just passing on a message. I have two appointment slots available.'

'Give me the first one.'

'Can you make it at two o'clock today?'

I swallow. Today! They want me to come in today! Shit! How urgent is this situation? I feel cold inside. 'Yes. My husband is busy all day. Can I come alone?'

'I'm afraid you have to come with your husband,' she insists.

'All right, we'll come in together.' My voice is a scared, foreign whisper.

'Good. I'll book you in.'

I don't run straight away to tell B.J. No, no, I won't frighten him unnecessarily. Suddenly I feel protective of him. He is so big and powerful, but I know that, on the inside, he would suffer far more than me. Mentally and emotionally, I am the stronger one. I will not show him my fear. Maybe it is nothing. Or maybe it is just a little thing.

She had sounded so serious though.

I touch my belly. Whatever it is, we will see it through. I walk into the kitchen and look around me. Everything looks the same. But it's as bewildering as a dream landscape. Perhaps I am still asleep. I blink and take a large breath. My hand flies up to my mouth to shut off the scream that wants to escape.

I walk to the island and I have the distinct sensation of weightlessness, as if I can float away like a helium balloon. I grab hold of the edge of the granite counter. I am gripping it so hard my knuckles show white. I stare at them with fascination. I am in such a state of shock I can't actually think. My mind is a complete blank. I take another deep breath and exhale noisily. It could be a mistake. That must be it. It happens all the time. I cling to the thought.

'It's most probably a mistake,' I whisper to myself.

I walk to the phone and dial Jake's number. He's always solved all my problems for me. I listen to the blurred sound of the rings in a daze. I terminate the call at the

third ring and put the phone back down on the table. It's silly to call him. I'll call him when I know more.

'Oh God!'

Did they detect an abnormality during the scan? I wrap my arms around my stomach. Tears gather in my eyes and spill down my cheeks. 'I love you. I don't care if you are disabled or anything. I'm here for you. You chose me and I chose you. No matter what, you are coming into this fucked up world.'

A smile comes to my face.

'You're coming into this family, boy,' I say fiercely. Strange how loud and strong my voice has become. 'Nothing. Nothing is going to stop you from being born. I'll protect you with my dying breath,' I promise.

I go to the mirror and wipe my eyes. I smile at my reflection.

'*Are you with me?*' the melodious voice of Lost Frequencies asks.

Yeah, I'm with you. I'm your mother. I'll always be with you no matter what. Come, let's go tell Daddy that you are super special.'

I walk along the corridor and stop in front of the gym. I pause and compose myself. When I open the door, BJ turns to look at me. His face is instantly concerned. I never disturb him while he is training. He puts the dumb bells he is working with down.

'What's up?'

I start walking towards him and immediately his large strides eat the distance between us and he envelops me in his arms.

'What's wrong?' he asks with a frown.

I attempt to smile, but from the expression on his face, I don't think I pull it off. 'The hospital called. There might be something wrong with our ...,' I take a deep breath and, though I try to hold the tears back, my eyes fill up, '...baby.'

'What?' He stares at me, his eyes wide and blank with horror.

I start to babble, the words hurried and stumbling over each other. 'It's all right. I think I'm all right with it. He's come to the right home. You and I will love him more than any other mummy or daddy, right?'

'What the fuck are you talking about?' he asks. He is white under his tan and he is staring at me as if he has never looked at me properly before.

The tears start running freely down my face. 'There's something wrong with our baby.'

'No,' he snarls and pulls me into his arms. He holds me so tight I make a strangled sound. He lets go of me instantly. 'Sorry, I didn't mean to hurt you,' he whispers.

'You didn't.'

He stares at me in shock and disbelief. 'Could they have made a mistake?'

You cannot imagine how much hope that hopeless question gives me. I throw my arms around him and hug him tightly. 'I was thinking exactly the same thing.'

We hold each other for I don't know how long. Both unwilling to look the other in the eye, and stop pretending that it is all a huge mistake. Eventually, I know it will have to be me. I know that this tiny little life is mine to steer. I pull away.

'I was counting back the other day and I know we conceived him on our very first night together. Whether they are wrong or right, we're having this baby, right? He chose us to be his parents, right?' I sniff.

He pulls me close to him and groans, 'Oh, Layla. Of course, we are. He's ours no matter what.'

We drive to the doctor's in complete silence, both of us terrified of what awaits us at the hospital. A nurse shows us to Dr. Freedman's office. We walk into his room hand-in-hand behind her. Dr. Freedman is a tall, bespectacled man. He looks up and smiles tightly. He is ill at ease.

'Mr. and Mrs. Pilkington. Please, have a seat,' he says politely indicating a set of blue chairs opposite him and letting his eyes slide away to some papers on his desk.

It is a surreal moment. I don't fear. I know in my DNA that, no matter what, I will protect my baby. I'm so aware of this moment that I can actually feel and experience everything. I sense the doctor's discomfort. I feel BJ's fear seeping out of his pores like something alive and tangible. I hear the faint sounds of people walking down the corridor. For them, it's a normal day. But for me, I can taste the disinfectant that the doctor used after the patient before us.

I can do this. I sit down and turn my head to watch BJ take the seat next to me. It hits me that this is a much bigger deal for him. I am clear in my head. No one. No one. No one can shake me. I turn to face the doctor.

The doctor's eyes are weary. He has done this too many times and is clearly dreading the task at hand. I smell his abhorrence of what he is about to say. Wordlessly, he pushes a box of tissues towards me.

I frown and look at BJ. His beautiful mouth opens and closes. And we realize that something is not just wrong. It is horribly wrong. It is worse, far worse than what I have imagined. Oh no.

NO. NO. NO

My darling BJ. So powerful and yet at this moment, felled. I reach my hand out and he envelops it in his own. I smile at him. He does not smile back.

'What's wrong with my baby?' I ask.

Dr. Freedman coughs and clears his throat. Behind him, I can see a poster of a skinless human body with all its veins showing.

'There's nothing wrong with your baby,' he says. 'It's you.' He says this gently and neutrally, but the room swings wildly.

THIRTY-TWO

Layla

'There's no easy way to say this. The ultrasound you had on the 15ᵗʰ showed that you either have endometrial cancer or hyperplasia that will likely rapidly progress to cancer. I'm so sorry.'

The unexpectedness of what he says is so great that I don't react at all. I feel myself go blank and numb. The big C? Me? Impossible. I'm born under a lucky star. I've been so spoilt. So sheltered. So fortunate. It's just not possible.

'What the fuck are you talking about? Can you fucking talk English?' BJ erupts aggressively.

Dr. Freedman shifts uncomfortably in his chair. It's obvious that he is not used to being spoken to so rudely. It is only BJ's size or pity that keeps him for retaliating. 'Your wife has a large mass in her uterus. It surrounds the baby on the top and sides. The rapid growth from total absence at the dating scan to what it was yesterday, makes me strongly suspect that it is certainly malignant and aggressively so. You should have been told at the ultrasound session yesterday, but the sonographer wanted to run the scans by me before making such a drastic diagnosis.'

'You're saying my wife has cancer?' BJ asks in disbelief.

'Yes.'

BJ jumps up so suddenly and with such force that his chair crashes to the ground. He slams his hand on the desk, his black eyes boring into the doctor's, and shouts, 'No, this a fucking mistake. How do you know the test results haven't been mislabeled? You do those fucking tests again.'

'Please, Mr. Pilkington. Sit down and calm down. This outburst is not going to help your wife.'

I reach out blindly for BJ's hand. His hand closes over mine. I look up at him. 'Please, BJ,' I whisper. For a second he doesn't respond. 'Please,' I beg again.

He picks the chair off the floor, rights it, and sits down. I notice that his hands are shaking. He fists his right hand and covers it with his left hand.

'The treatment for cancer and hyperplasia to the extent I saw on the ultrasound,' the doctor continues, 'is immediate hysterectomy to stage and figure out the prognosis.'

'A hysterectomy?' I gasp.

The doctor shifts uncomfortably. 'I'm afraid so.'

'You want to take her womb out?' BJ repeats in disbelief. 'What the fuck! She's 23 years old, for the love of God!'

'I'm sorry,' the doctor says lamely.

BJ lunges forward suddenly. 'If you say you're sorry one more fucking time, I swear, I'll give you something to be sorry about. This is a mistake, pure and simple.'

The doctor's eyes bulge with fear. He leans backwards and places his hands on the armrests of his chair, as if he is getting ready to bolt. 'I know you are very upset, but I have personally gone through all the results and I can assure you, Mr. Pilkington, that there is no mistake.'

I glance at BJ and I see by his crushed expression that he knows the doctor is telling the truth. BJ has used violence to solve every problem in his life. He has never encountered a scenario that he couldn't win using brute force alone. But for the first time his fists are of no use. He is totally helpless. And it scares him.

'Is there another way? A way to save the baby?' I whisper.

'I'm very sor—.' The doctor stops mid-word and glances nervously at BJ. 'I'm afraid there is no way to save your baby. I must recommend immediate termination of the pregnancy.'

'What happens if I don't do anything?'

BJ has fallen eerily silent. He is cradling his head in his hands.

The doctor frowns. 'First of all you will be greatly endangering your own life. It's not a risk that's worth taking since the lack of room will mean your placenta will be on your cervix. With the weight of the baby and the tumor, you would be at a high risk for a placental abruption.'

I exhale the breath I was holding. 'What is that?' I ask.

'It's when the placenta peels away from the inner wall of the uterus before delivery. It deprives the baby of oxygen and causes heavy bleeding in the mother. It can be fatal to both mother and child.'

'I still want a second opinion,' BJ says with a deadly calm that's more frightening than his furious outburst before.

The doctor nods calmly. 'I have already arranged for your wife to see the head of OB and a maternal fetal specialist at 9:00 the day after tomorrow. They'll do another ultrasound with better equipment and they will also perform an ultrasound biopsy.'

'Is the ultrasound biopsy safe for my baby?' I ask.

The doctor looks pained. 'They will be able to stay away from the baby and the sac, but the chances for a spontaneous miscarriage afterwards exist. I would recommend an immediate termination.'

I stand up abruptly. 'All right. Thank you, doctor,' I say, and look down at BJ.

He gazes up at me. He looks so confused and lost I want to take him to my breast. He stands slowly. It's obvious he is not ready to leave, as if discussing it further could change anything.

We walk out of the doctor's office and cross the car park like two survivors of a war. Hanging on to each other. Seeing nothing around us. Shell-shocked. Devastated. BJ unlocks the car and opens the passenger door for me. I slide into the seat in silence. He gets in, closes the door, and puts the keys in the ignition, but does not start the engine.

I turn to him. He looks as dazed and bewildered as the moths that fly into light bulbs and fall to the floor, lying on their backs, they slowly wheel their legs into the arms of death.

'Can you believe it?' I ask.

'Oh, baby,' he croaks. 'I think I just need to hold you for a second.'

I throw myself at him and sob my heart out in the bleak hospital car park.

We drive home in heavy silence, both of us locked in our own pain. When we reach our home, I stare ahead of me blankly. I simply cannot summon the energy to open the car door and go into the house.

He opens my door and holds his hand out to me. With a sigh I put my hand in his and let him haul me upright.

Mrs. Roberts from next door meets us on the pavement.

'Are you all right, dear?'

I nod automatically. 'Thank you. Yes.'

She stares at us with a baffled expression as BJ helps me up the steps. He opens the door and we enter our silent home.

'Do you want to lie down for a bit, babe?' he asks me.

I nod. 'Yes, that's a good idea. But can I have a glass of water first?'

'Of course.' He seems glad to be of use. I watch him stride away towards the kitchen. Thank god it is Nora's, my housekeeper, day off. I couldn't bear to see anyone else. BJ comes back with a glass of water and I drink it all and give him the empty glass. He puts it on the nearest surface and comes back to me.

We climb the stairs together. When we reach the bed a great exhaustion swamps

me and I sit heavily on the mattress. He crouches down and gently takes my shoes off. I look down at him, at the way his luxurious eyelashes sweep down to his cheeks, and a crazy, totally inappropriate thought pops into my head. I want to have sex with him. For a second there is intense guilt and then the consoling thought. It's not crazy. It's just instinct. My body has no intellect of its own. Every time it's near him, it just wants to copulate.

I close my eyes and let the instinct slink away in shame. Tenderly he kisses my palms and closed eyelids. Then he stands up and I lie down. Quietly, he covers my body with the duvet.

'Thank you,' I say.

He nods gravely, draws the curtains closed and leaves the room, closing the door behind him. I hear him hesitate outside the door, then take a few steps, stop, come back to the door. But, after a pause, he goes downstairs.

I lie on the bed and stare at the ceiling in disbelief. My mind turns round and round desperately, like a rat in cage, trying to find a way out. There must be another way. Slowly my hands cup my belly. I hear BJ climb the stairs. I put my hands down and turn to my side, facing away from the door, and close my eyes.

He comes in and stands over me.

He knows I am awake. I feel him sit on the bed. 'I love you, Layla. Whatever happens I love only you. You're my life. Without you nothing else matters.' His voice breaks, but I don't open my eyes. Tears slip out of my closed eyelids.

'I'm going out now. There are things I need to sort out, but I'll be back in an hour. Just rest, OK?'

He kisses my head and then I hear his footsteps run down the stairs. I know then that he has made his decision, and he can live it. And now he is doing everything in his power to facilitate that decision. I wait until I hear the front door close before I get up. I walk out of our bedroom and turn right, heading to the nursery.

I open the door, seeing the cot that Lily and I bought, and the full horror of my situation hits me. My knees give way and I slump to the ground outside my baby's room. My arms pull tight across my body, as if I am cold. I realize that I am actually in a strange, dreaming state. It feels as if my heartbeat has slowed down.

In that oddly still moment, I remember my mother taking me to a tarot reader as a small child. As if it had happened yesterday, I clearly and distinctly remember her telling my mother, 'I cannot read her cards now, Mara. Her destiny is special. A great sacrifice will be asked of her. If I am still alive then, I will read her cards for her.'

Even as a small girl I had picked up her sense of unease and dread, reverberating on a level beyond language, beyond what is cognitive. I didn't even need to understand her to feel it.

'What do you mean?' my ma had asked.

But she would say no more.

I stumble down the stairs and find my purse. I root around in it with trembling hands and find my mobile phone. Taking a deep breath, I call my mother.

'Ma,' I say into the phone. It is shocking how level and even I manage to keep my voice. A few hours ago, I wouldn't have understood how anyone could appear unmoved when they are dying inside. Now I know. The cold, hard part of me has detached itself enough to be able to function without the rest of me. Appearing unmoved is the price you pay for being able to speak at all.

'Ah, I was just about to call you,' my mother says cheerfully.

'Why?'

'I'm in a shop and I've seen the cutest little coats you've ever seen. I'm getting a pink one for our Liliana. Shall I get a blue one for Tommy as well?'

It is like a body blow. The only way to deal with it is talk about something crazy. 'Why are you calling him Tommy, Ma?'

'BJ told me that both of you had decided on that name.'

An involuntary smile escapes my stiff features. Oh, BJ. How sly you are.

'Have you changed your mind then?' my mother asks.

'No. No, we haven't. We are going with Tommy. Yeah, get the blue coat for him,' I tell her.

'All right, I will. What did you call me for?'

'I wanted the phone number of that tarot card reader you always go to. I've forgotten her name.'

'Queenie, you mean?'

'Yeah, that's the one.'

'I'll text her number to you. Do you want to go and see her then?'

'Yes.'

'We can go together if you want.'

'No, Ma. I was planning on seeing her today.'

'Is anything wrong?'

'No. Nothing is wrong. Just wanted to ask her something.'

'She should be free now. She doesn't work on Mondays. Too quiet on the pier. I'll text her number to you now. Speak to you later tonight.'

'Thanks, Ma.'

The text comes through and I call Queenie and make an appointment to see her in an hour and a half. Then I send BJ a text message.

Got 2 run an errand.
Will go directly 2 Silver

 256

Lee after that. Call u
when I get there. xx

    I switch off my mobile, input Queenie's address into my GPS, and drive my car to her trailer park. I'm there in less than an hour. I get out of the car and begin to walk.

    The body remembers what the mind will not. My legs move confidently forward. My muscles and sinew know exactly where she lives. They always knew that one day I would be returning again to see the woman who could look into the future. She opens the door in her flowery housecoat. She is so small and shrunken. She is nothing like I remember.

    'Poor child. So soon you have been asked for your sacrifice,' she says sadly.

    My chin begins to tremble.

    She steps aside and I enter her trailer. She bids me to sit.

    'What do you want of me?' she asks.

    'Read my cards.'

THIRTY-THREE

Layla

Frogs in my belly devour what is bad.
Frogs in my belly show the evil the way out!
- Old gypsy witches' chant

By the time I arrive at Silver Lee, BJ's car is already parked in the forecourt. He comes tearing out to meet me, his hair tousled as if he has been running his hands through it and his eyes stormy with worry.

'Where have you been?' he demands.

I should feel guilty but I don't. The cold, hard part of me is still in charge. 'I went to see a friend of my mother.'

He stares at me in disbelief. 'What the fuck, Layla? I've been so worried. You switched off your phone. I didn't know how to reach you.'

'I'm sorry. I just needed a bit of time to think.'

'We need to talk.'

I put my hand out, the palm facing him. 'Not today.'

He opens his mouth to object and I say, 'Please, BJ. Tomorrow. We'll talk tomorrow.'

He looks at me warily. 'We *have* to talk. It's not going to go away, Layla.'

'One more day is not going to a make a difference,' I cry.

'All right. All right. Tomorrow. But it cannot be any later than tomorrow.'

'Thank you, BJ.' I look down at myself. 'I feel a bit grubby. I think I'll just have a shower first.'

He looks at me intently, but I ignore the look, I walk up to him and standing on tip-toes kiss him gently on the mouth before I go into the house. He stands where I have left him, staring after me with confusion.

'Hello, Layla,' Marcel calls cheerfully from the kitchen.

'Hey, Marcel,' I greet and go up the stairs.

I shower quickly, dress, and go downstairs. BJ is standing with his back to me looking out of the open windows. In one hand he is holding a glass of something amber, in the other a cigarette. An open bottle of Scotch is standing on the table. Its top is carelessly tossed on the table. I am wearing flat, soft-soled slippers and he has not heard me come down. For a moment I watch him. He's totally lost in thought, his powerful shoulders hunched forward and tense.

'I've never seen you drink Scotch before.'

He whirls around, his eyes narrowed, and running over me like water. 'Yeah, I needed something for my nerves.' He takes a long drag of his cigarette and kills it in the ashtray sitting on the window ledge. He straightens and looks at me. 'Do you want a glass of something?' he asks slowly.

I blink. There is a sharp pain in my heart. I haven't even had a sip of anything alcoholic since I found out I was pregnant and he has never offered before today.

We stare at each other.

'I'll have a glass of white wine,' I say softly.

He goes to the bar, selects a bottle from the fridge and pours me a glass.

I take it. Our hands touch, a spark runs through me.

Watching him over the rim of the wineglass, I take a sip. It feels cold on my tongue, but it doesn't taste too good. Perhaps I am not in the mood for it.

He picks up his own glass, taking a swallow, and looks at me with deliberately blank eyes. 'Want to tell me what you did this afternoon?'

I sit down on the sofa behind me. 'I went to see my mother's tarot reader.'

'Right,' he says carefully. 'What did she tell you?'

'Not much. Nothing that would help, anyway.' I stare down at the floor

'We'll have other children, Layla. I promise.'

My head shoots up and my eyes are stern. 'I don't want to discuss it today. Please, BJ.'

'Fine.' There is a note of frustration in his voice.

I put my glass of wine down on the coffee table and clasp my hands.

'Shall we go for a walk?' BJ asks.

'Yes, let's.'

We don't walk far. Both of us turning back as soon as we reach the end of the lane that leads into the forest. When we come back, dinner is ready and we eat it—well, push it around our plates—on the roof terrace in strained silence. Afterwards, we go upstairs, fuck like animals, and fall asleep entwined in each other's arms.

The last thing I hear is his voice whispering in my ear, 'God, if anything ever happened to you.'

I wake up in the early hours of the morning. One of the windows is open and a light breeze is coming in. Very quietly I get out of bed, slipping my nightgown over my head as I head for the nursery. The curtains are open and it's bathed in moonlight. I open one of the tall windows and sit on the deep ledge with my legs dangling out. Down below the rose bushes are in full bloom. Their heads are so big they look like cabbages in the dark. In the distance the enormous weeping willow is very still. Its sad branches trailing on the ground.

I hear a noise behind me. I don't turn around.

'Can't sleep?' he asks.

I shake my head. He comes and stands behind me and I feel the heat from his body.

'I don't think I like you sitting on the ledge like that. You could fall.'

I look up at him. In the moonlight his face looks like it is carved out of mahogany.

'I won't,' I tell him quietly.

He sits next to me, but faces the room. I turn my head and look into his eyes.

'It's already tomorrow. We need to talk, Layla.'

'OK, let's talk.'

'We need a second opinion. I've made an appointment tomorrow afternoon with a specialist, an oncologist. He's the best in England.'

'I see.'

'If he confirms the diagnosis then we'll go ahead with the termination immediately and begin your treatment.'

I drop my head.

'Layla?'

I look up. 'And you're all right with us never having children?'

He does not hesitate. 'Yes.' His voice is very clear.

'I'm not,' I say.

'Then we will adopt. There are enough children around crying out for a good home.'

He has everything figured out. I touch his dear face. 'I'm not terminating the baby, BJ.'

THIRTY-FOUR

Layla

He becomes still under my hand. 'What the fuck are you talking about?'

I take my hand away from his face and hug myself. 'I'm not giving up my baby. He's perfectly healthy and it's not fair that he should lose his life just because I am ill.'

He stands suddenly and begins to pace. I retract my legs and turn to face him. He stops in front of me. His face is pale.

There's a white line around his lips. He is furious. He looks like he wants to shake me.

'You don't seem to get it. If you have this baby you're going to die, Layla.'

'Could die,' I correct.

He throws his hands up in disbelief. 'Were you not in the doctor's office with me? Did you not hear the terminology he used? Aggressively malignant. A risk not worth taking. Placental abruption. Pregnancy will not survive.'

'Then let it terminate on its own. Murdering my own child goes against every instinct and belief I have. I couldn't do that and carry on living.'

He is so shocked he takes a step back. 'Jesus, Layla. This is not murder. It's a fetus, yet unborn. It has no concept of being alive. It only exists. You on the other hand are alive and loved by so many people, living a charmed life.'

'Are you telling me that life can go on being charmed for me after I kill my child? Can you promise that I won't wake up in a cold sweat in the middle of the night because I've heard my baby crying? Or that for the rest of my life I won't be wondering what he would have grown up to be?'

He stares at me in open-mouthed horror.

'How will I ever stop mourning for my innocent child if I am the one who caused his death? It will be a bloody stain on my soul.'

'In that case, you don't need to make this decision. I will. Let it be a stain on my soul.'

I stand up and walk to him. 'This baby belongs to us, but at this moment it is in my body, and I'll defend it to my last breath.'

'Do you really believe that this child will grow up happy knowing that it killed its own mother?'

'No, he will grow up feeling that his mother loved him so much she gave up her life so that he could live. What a beautiful thought to carry through life. What richness!'

'I cannot believe what you are saying. You're really are just a spoilt child who wants what she wants, after all. Damn the consequences for everyone else,' he accuses brutally.

I shake my head. 'Yes, it's true that all my life, I've been spoilt and given everything I've ever wanted. All I had to do was ask for it and it appeared. And I lived like a princess, untouched by suffering, never giving more than a passing thought to all the misery in this world: the starving children in Africa, the wretched Palestinians in the Gaza strip, the pitiful child slaves in China who make my fashionable trainers, and the countless abuses that goes on in this big, unfair world. But, you see, I've never been asked to make a difference. I never even thought I could. This is the first time I am being asked. I know it's a big ask, but I'm up to it.'

'Who do you think you are now? Fucking Buddha?'

'I don't think that. I just know this baby came to me. And I'm not killing it.'

'So you're going to let it kill you instead?' he asks.

'It's not written in stone that I'll die if I have this baby. Doctors can be wrong. I'm going to do everything in my power to be well.'

'And how are you going to do that?' he snaps.

'I'm going to take all the holistic measures I can to keep the cancer at bay until the baby is big enough to survive outside my body. While Lily was pregnant I found out a lot from her about eating well and how the right foods and herbs can cure and keep at bay so many diseases. And during Lily's confinement period, I learned even more from her grandmother.'

'This is pure madness. You're talking about using herbs to fight cancer!'

'Don't twist my words. My plan is more far reaching than you are making it out to be.'

'I won't let you, Layla.'

'You can't stop me, BJ. No one can. My mind's made up.'

'What if this was happening to me? How would you feel then?'

I frown. I had not given it a thought. 'To be honest, I would probably react the way you are, but the thing is, I'm not you. I'm me, Layla. The only person this baby has fighting its corner. He chose me to be his mother. To live inside me until he is able to survive in this world on his own, and I'm not turning my back on him.'

'I don't want this baby without you,' he snarls suddenly.

Both my hands rush to cover my stomach protectively, as if he has administered a blow to my unborn child.

He shakes his head sadly. 'I couldn't love him, Layla. Not if he kills you. Every time I'd see him, I'd know you're not here because of him.'

I smile. 'You know what, I'm not afraid you won't love him. You will. Because he is a part of you and me.'

He closes his eyes. When he opens them they are pained. 'I'm sorry, but I can't do this, Layla. Other men may be able to do it because they don't love their wives the way I love you. I just can't. I can't stand by and watch you throw your life away, not even my own child. I can't choose him over you. I can't. I just can't. And you can't fucking ask me to.'

'All we have to do is hold on for another three months. Actually, it's not even three months. It's only 77 days before he will be 25 weeks and can be safely delivered via cesarean section.'

'You don't have three months. Don't you get what aggressively malignant means? It would have eaten into you by then. You need to cut it out now or it will be too late.'

'I *know* I can hold on for 77 days. We'll make a calendar and cross the days off together, OK?'

He looks up to the ceiling and exhales. 'Don't try and pacify me, Layla. You can't. I feel all torn up. I couldn't care for this child ... not without you. You'll be giving birth to an orphan.'

I put my finger on his lips. 'Shhh ... don't speak anymore. I want to call our baby Tommy.'

He buries his head in his hands and I put my hand on his head running my fingers through the silky black hair.

'I hope he has black hair,' I whisper.

He says nothing.

'I hope he looks like you.'

His body jerks.

'I love you, BJ.'

He looks up at me bitterly. 'Fuck you, Layla.'

'I love you, BJ.'

'With a love like yours, I don't need enemies,' he cries in an anguished voice, and strides out of the room.

I hear him run down the steps, then the front door slams. I turn to the window and see him rush towards his car. He opens his car door and suddenly looks up at me. We stare at each other. He drags his eyes away, slamming his car door and speeding away, the wheels spinning on the gravel.

I sit on the windowsill to wait for him.

It seems as if ages pass. I am sitting with my head leaning against the glass when I hear the powerful roar of his car. He parks, looks up to the window, sees me, and begins to run. I hear him take the steps three maybe four at time. He bursts through the door and crossing the room takes me into his arms.

'You're freezing,' he says. His voice throbs with emotion.

'I was waiting for you.'

'What did that tarot reader say to you?'

I lift my face away from his chest. 'She said I was born holding three lives in my hand. Mine, the baby's, and yours.'

'I love you more than life itself, so I am telling you now, I'll do everything in my power to stop you from having this baby.'

THIRTY-FIVE

Layla

'**L**ayla, of course, we're all utterly and completely torn up about the baby, but we simply can't let you do this. You can't expect us to. We love you. You can't do this to us, to BJ,' Jake says gently.

I look at them one by one: my mother, Jake, Dominic, and Shane. For the last hour and a half they have taken turns, alternately shouting, coaxing, wheedling, and threatening to force me to change my mind.

At different times, they have all looked at me as if I have gone completely crazy. Maybe I am crazy. All I know is that Tommy came to me, and asked me to be his mother. I agreed and I'm not going back on my word.

'I'm not changing my mind. You can either help me by finding out all the ways I can naturally hold the cancer at bay for the next 76 days or you can just stand by and watch me do it alone,' I repeat my stand again.

I look at them all calmly.

Jake shakes his head in disbelief, throwing his arms up into the air and striding off angrily. I know he will be back. Jake doesn't give up easy, but I *have* won this round.

As ever, it is soft-hearted Dominic who cracks first. 'All right. I will help you. Tell me what you want me to do and I'll do it.'

Gratefully, I rush to him and hug him tightly. 'Thank you. Thank you so much, Dom. You don't know what this means to me,' I say, tears stinging my eyes.

Next to capitulate is Shane. I squeeze both his hands. But my mother just sits there like a statue, tears pouring down her face.

'Leave me for a bit with Ma,' I tell my brothers. They leave the room silently and close the door.

I don't talk to my mother. I go and sit next to her, hold her hands, and look into her eyes. And suddenly we start crying. Both of us just weeping.

'How could this happen to you?' she sobs. 'You're my baby. Without you there is no joy in this family.'

'Then help me beat this,' I choke back.

'How?'

I wipe my eyes. 'I've already done a bit of research on the net this morning, but I'm going to do more. The plan is to keep myself so healthy that the cancer cannot advance at any great speed. I only have to keep it at bay for 76 days,' I tell her passionately.

I see a trembling ray of hope shine into my mother's eyes. '76 days?'

I nod. 'Just 76 days, Ma. That's not much to give up for a whole baby, is it?'

My mother covers her mouth with her hand and shakes her head.

I sigh with relief.

She uncovers her mouth. 'I'm so proud of you, Layla. You've really grown up good.'

I could have gone home and done my research there on my on laptop, but I want to include her, so we go upstairs to the desktop computer that she never uses and pour over cancer research together. We stay clear of allopathic treatments or websites that don't have any endorsement by serious doctors or researchers. In two hours, we've printed reams and reams of research material. We split the papers into two piles. Ma takes one and I take the other.

It is nearly lunchtime when I lift my head from the article I am studying. BJ is waiting for me at home. For as long as I can remember, my mother has always stood in the kitchen surrounded by food when I left the house. Today, she is wearing her reading glasses and the kitchen table is full of papers.

I look at my mother and I feel a great sadness. I pull myself together. I cannot afford, even for a second, to reflect on or question my decision. It will bring fear into my body and sap away my strength.

'Bye, Ma,' I say, kissing the top of her head.

She grabs me, hugs me tightly, and follows me out of the house. Her forlorn figure waves to me from the front door.

THIRTY-SIX

Layla

"Let food be thy medicine and medicine be thy food."
— Hippocrates, recognized as the father of modern medicine

I arrive home and find BJ up on the roof terrace. He glances at me and carries on staring out at the landscape.

'Hey,' I say and sit beside him.

'Hey yourself,' he replies. There is something in his voice that makes me turn and look at him closely.

'What have you been up to?' I ask.

He kicks at something by his feet and an empty bottle of Scotch rolls out and hits the table leg.

'I see.'

'I've confirmed the appointment for the scan and biopsy tomorrow at nine in the morning,' he says.

'I'm not going.'

'Yeah? Why not?' His voice is vaguely aggressive, as if he is just getting started.

'Because there is no point, is there? All that will happen is they'll confirm what Dr. Freedman said and increase the chances of the pregnancy terminating.'

'Jesus, this just gets worse and worse,' he mutters furiously.

I touch his arm. 'BJ? Remember when you said you'd do anything for me?'

He closes his eyes, the anger dying out of him.

'I really need you to do something for me now.'

He opens his eyes. They are so black they are like holes in his sad face. 'I want to tell you something,' he says quietly.

'OK.'

He looks at me, his face twisted with bitterness. 'It's not going to be pretty.'

I don't speak. It is as if the air is made of the most delicate glass, cold and breakable. I feel scared. There is already so much on my plate and I am afraid I will not be able to cope with whatever he is going to tell me. My head inclines so slightly it's almost not perceptible.

'I've never told anyone. I don't even allow myself to think it.'

I stare at him, hardly daring to breathe.

'Do you want to know why I fight? Why I used to be so goddamn crazy in the pit that I almost killed a man once?'

I remember the way he had attacked his opponent in the pit. It was vicious and merciless. A light breeze ruffles his hair and drops it to his forehead. His eyes are vulnerable and defenseless. Yes, I can handle anything about him. Anything. I nod.

'At my birth, my mother was incorrectly told to push before she was fully dilated. It ruptured her cervix and she lost the ability to ever again carry a child to full term. After that, she lost four children: A boy at 18 weeks, a set of twins—a boy and a girl—at 22 weeks, and another girl at 21 weeks. There were others that fell out as lumps of blood in the toilet. It ruined her life.'

I shiver at the thought.

'My father had a smile identical to mine. Everybody thought so. They also thought he was the perfect father. No one knew that he blamed me for the deaths of my siblings, or that he often battered me senseless.'

I stare at him in shock.

He smiles bitterly. 'Yup. He had hands like raw meaty hunks. Broke my jaw twice, he did. He claimed he was toughening me up, but I think he enjoyed it. Abusing me was entertainment for him. I understood what he wanted early on. He wanted to see me cry. I'd be screaming inside, but I never cried. I kept it all inside. All the rage. All the pain. All the hurt.'

'Oh, BJ,' I gasp.

'From the time I was fifteen, I'd walk around looking for a fight. I'd walk into a bar or a club, and all it took for the rage to take over, for me to send a guy to the hospital, was a wrong look. Any provocation, no matter how small or insignificant, was enough to fill my guts with fury. I was a ticking time bomb.

'It poisoned my bloodstream. Every once in a while I had to let it out in a safe environment. Like a bloodletting. Stress relief. Every victory in the pit was a victory of my vulnerable, younger self over my father.'

I frown with confusion. 'Then why did you tell me you trusted your father?'

'I did. I trusted him to hurt me. He showed me the face that no one else saw.'

'And your mother. Did she know?'

'She knew. There was nothing she could do, but pretend. We both pretended.'

'What happened to you is absolutely horrific, but why do I sense that you're linking it with our child?'

'I'm the spitting image of my father. I'm gonna batter that boy, Layla. I'm not going to be able to help it.'

I freeze. 'You're *not* your father,' I whisper.

'You don't know that. Even I don't know what's inside me. His brutality created a monster.'

'Oh my great, big hero, my heart, my love, you're not your father. You'll never be him. I don't have even a second of worry that you'll batter our Tommy. Not for one second. Your father was a monster. I know you're not.'

He drops his gaze. 'I don't love this life enough to stay on without you. If you go, I want to go with you.'

I crouch in front of him. 'Listen to me. I don't plan to go anywhere. I really think I can do it. Other people have. I've been on the Internet all morning with Ma doing research. I've found out that people are fighting their cancers by all kinds of methods.'

He looks at me and I see how much he wants to believe me, but he is afraid to take the risk. He wants to take the riskless path.

'Cancer is not a disease I caught from dirty water or someone else. My own body made it. So even if they cut it all out, if I live in exactly the same way I have been doing until now, my body is going to make it again.'

'I feel so fucking helpless.'

I smile softly. 'Well, you're not as helpless as you think.'

He looks at me curiously.

'This is going to make you laugh, but you know how I said I wanted you to get out of the drug business? Well, looks like I'm going to need you to get back into it. I need you to supply me with marijuana.'

His eyes widen.

'I need the fresh leaves and buds. And I need loads.'

He frowns. 'For what?'

'Apparently the marijuana leaf is a highly medicinal substance. Besides being antioxidant, anti-inflammatory, and neuro-protective, it possesses an anti-cancer nutrient compound known as cannabinoid. Cannabinoid is capable of many wonders, but the most exciting thing about it, is its ability to normalize cell communication within the body. It bridges the gap of neurotransmission in the central nervous system and brain by providing a two-way system of communication, a positive feedback loop. So for people like me, whose systems are compromised by rogue cancer cells, a positive feedback loop can be established.'

'So you're going to be high the whole time.'

I shake my head. 'No, heat is needed to convert the THCA element of raw cannabis into THC, which creates the high. I'm going to juice raw marijuana leaves and buds and eat salads of hemp sprouts.'

'I really want to believe that raw cannabis is going to cure you, but I have to say, it sounds really far-fetched.'

'First off, marijuana is only one of the things in a whole host of measures that I will be taking. Cancer cells need an acidic environment to grow. So I'm also going to keep my system alkaline. And I'm going to cut out GMOs and pesticides, go vegetarian, completely cut out stress, etcetera. Here, look at this.' I open my bag, flicking through the papers to find the article I am looking for and put it into his hand. He looks at it eagerly.

'Check this out,' I say. 'Even though US federal government officials consistently deny that marijuana has any medical benefits, the government actually holds patents since October 2003 for 26 methods using cannabinoids as antioxidants and neuroprotectants.' I point my finger at the paper and say, 'See, US Patent 6630507?'

He looks up at me, almost believing, but not quite.

I grab both his hands. 'You have to believe me. I can do this.'

He sighs heavily.

'Even people suffering from end-stage cancer have benefited,' I say.

281

'OK, Layla. OK. I'll get the marijuana for you.' He stares at me. 'And I'll join you in your new diet.'

'Oh, my darling. You don't have to do that. You'll hate it. My diet will be filled with alfalfa grass, sprouts, kefir, and all manner of horrible stuff.'

'What the hell is kefir?'

'It's an organism that you put in milk to sour it and turn it into a probiotic food.'

He winces at the thought.

I laugh. 'Hey. I don't need you to go on the diet with me. I need you to eat what you want and be happy. When you are happy, I feel happy. And when I'm happy my body is happy.'

'So. You're gonna cook separately for me?'

'Why not? My food is going to be mostly raw anyway.'

'But you'll have to smell my food.'

'So what?'

He nods slowly. 'No. I wanna do the diet with you.'

'It won't make any difference to me.'

'It'll make a difference to me. We eat the same or I don't eat at all.'

'OK.' And I have to blink back the tears.

THIRTY-SEVEN

BJ

This morning I watched her tick the box on our calendar that held the sacred information: 60 days left. She turned to me bright and so full of hope. So I went to work. I called her a few times. She seemed fine. But when I return home at 7:00, she is in bed.

> I rush to her. 'What's wrong?'
> 'It's nothing. Just a twinge.'
> 'What kind of a twinge?'

'It's normal. Even Lily used to get little twinges and stuff. Don't worry, the baby is OK,' she reassures.

I lose it then. She mistakes my expression of blind rage for fear. 'Don't worry, darling. There'll probably be many more such days.'

'What the fuck is the matter with you?' I roar. 'How can you do this to yourself?'

Taken aback by my fury, she tries to fluff over the utter madness of what she is doing. 'Darling,' she says. 'I'm all right. Really. I'm only lying in bed to ease the stress on my cervix.'

'Of course you are. Obviously, you don't want to go to the hospital and get a real doctor's opinion.'

She shifts. 'No, I don't.'

'That's just great,' I throw at her. In complete despair, I leave the house. I hear her call out to me, but what's the fucking point? She's just going to explode my head with more nonsense.

I get into the car, start the engine, and drive blindly. In the end, I find myself driving to one of Dominic's clubs. The valet jumps into my car and radios the staff in the reception. They wave me through. At reception there are more wide smiles, and of course, there is no entrance fee for me to pay. A pretty girl lifts the curtain and I enter Heat Exchange. The housemother comes towards me with a large smile.

'We haven't seen you for a while,' she says softly. 'We've had a really nice blonde girl join us. Anastasia is Russian. Beautiful body.'

I nod and she leads me towards a booth. It is early and there is hardly anybody in it. A girl is on stage gyrating. She has long dark hair. Something about her reminds me of Layla. I quickly look away.

I sit in the booth. A waitress comes. 'The usual?' she asks.

'No. Get me a bottle of rum.'

'Of course.'

A blonde girl, obviously Anastasia, sashays towards me. She is bite-your-arm-off beautiful and there is only one way to describe her body. Roger Rabbit's girlfriend's statuesque. She stops in front me and strikes a pose to show her body to its full advantage.

'Hey, big boy,' she says throatily.

'Hello.'

'You want a dance?'

'Sure,' I say and put a twenty pound note on the table and push it a few inches away from me.

She smiles, takes it, and pushes it into her garter. And then she starts dancing. At first keeping her distance and then getting closer and closer until her breasts are either a hair's breath away from me or accidentally brushing me. She times her five minutes with precision.

'Do you want to buy me a drink?'

'Why not?' I signal for the waitress.

'A glass of champagne,' she tells the waitress and turns her glance back to me.

'So, you have a clubs of your own?'

I nod.

'If I need a job, I can come to you?'

'No. I don't deal with that side of the business.'

'Of course. You are too busy.'

I find I can't be bothered to talk. I let my eyes travel down her body. She gets it straight away. 'You want to go to the VIP room?' she asks.

'Sure,' I tell her. We walk to the VIP room together, Roger Rabbit's girlfriend and me, but inside I am dying.

Layla

I dream that I am bleeding, that blood is gushing out of me. I try to staunch the flow with my hand and it oozes between my fingers. I feel myself become lighter and lighter and I float out of my body. I look down at myself, a corpse. I want to reach out and touch my own body. In my dream I think, *this is what I will look like when I die.* Then I wake up. I look at the alarm clock. It is almost midnight and BJ is not home. I call his phone, but it is switched off. I leave a message and call his manager. He has not been there all night. I try all the other places he could be. No luck. So I call Jake.

'Am I disturbing you?' I ask softly.

'No. What is it?' There is a wire of panic in his voice. In the background I can hear music.

'I can't find BJ. Is he there?'

I hear the relief in his voice. 'He's not here.'

'I'm worried about him. We ... we argued. He stormed out.'

There is a moment of silence. Then Jake's voice comes on. It is calm and business like. 'I take it you've already tried all his restaurants and clubs.'

'Yes,' I reply holding the phone with both my hands.

'I think I know where he is. Don't worry. It'll be all right. I'll call you a bit later. Get some rest, OK?'

Jake Eden

I end the call and look at my phone.

'What's wrong?' Lily asks worriedly.

I turn towards her voice gratefully. God, I cannot imagine what it must be like for BJ. If it was Lily I'd have to ... I walk up to her and kiss her. 'That was Layla. BJ is MIA and she's worried, but I think I know where he is. I don't know how long this will take so don't wait up for me, OK?

'I will wait up for you.'

I smile. 'Wear something special for me.'

'You bet.'

'Right, I'm off.'

'Give him a big kiss from me,' Lily says.

'You've always liked him, haven't you?'

'Yes, I've never forgotten that he saved your life.'

I don't say anything, but memories flood back into my mind.

There is no traffic on the roads and it takes me less than an hour to drive down to the coast to where the old smuggler's network of caves are. I know BJ used to go there many years ago. Once I stumbled upon him. We were still enemies then, but he was very drunk and he offered me a drink. We shared a bottle, but he was so plastered I don't think he has any memory of that night. If he has, he's never referred to it.

As soon as I turn off the road and drive down the dirt track, I spot his vehicle. I stop the car and text Layla.

Found him. All is well. Will make sure he gets home safe.

My poor sister must have been watching the phone like a hawk. She texts back almost instantly.

Thank u from the bottom of my heart. xxxx

I take my torchlight out of my car's glove compartment and go into the mouth of the cave. It is dark and dry. My shoes sink into the soft sand. After a while, the soft sand gives way to rock and I start to hear the sound of water dripping. A few yards later I come to the flooded area of the cave. I take my shoes and socks off and rollup my pants, then wade through the water.

When I reach dry stone, I put my socks and shoes back on and walk for another ten minutes or so through the twisting tunnel. It opens out to sheer drop into the sea. BJ is sitting at the end of it. He's so heavily slumped he looks like a rock in the darkness. He has an oil lamp beside him. I switch off my torch. As far as the eye can see is the ocean. In the moonlight, it glistens like a black, oily mass. Arching over it, the sky is a blanket of stars.

I notice that he's barefoot. He must not have bothered to put his shoes back on. I sit at the edge beside him and let my feet dangle down. He is holding a bottle of rum.

'Layla was worried about you,' I say.

He passes the bottle over to me. I take a swallow and return it. He takes a swig and wedges it between his thighs.

'It's funny, isn't it? There was a time I wished I knew what it was like to be with her, even for a moment. I guess I got my fucking wish. So I can't complain too much.'

I take the bottle of rum from him and take a huge mouthful.

He turns towards me. 'If you carry on like this you won't be able to drive me back to her. That's what you're here for, isn't it?'

'That's true. That's what she wanted from me.'

'And what Layla wants, Layla gets,' he says bitterly.

I frown. 'At first I, too, wanted her to terminate the pregnancy, but now I understand that she is making a moral decision. And that is her right. I can't force her. She wants to do the right thing, the thing that she can be proud of. I didn't realize my sister was such a little hero.'

He takes another swig and stares at me bleary-eyed. 'Yeah. I know. I want to support our little hero and everything, but I can't. You see, I only ever wanted her. I cannot ever remember a time when I've wanted another. All my life, I was waiting for her. And now she wants me to give her the OK to go and risk her life for a fetus that has a high probability of spontaneously miscarrying anyway. How the hell can I be expected to support that?'

'What will happen if you don't support her and ... something happens?'

He makes a sound. A grunt of deep pain. 'Something? Define something.'

I remain silent. It's impossible to say the words.

'Here's a question for you, then. What if it was Lily this was happening to?'

I grab the bottle and glug down so fast I have a coughing fit. BJ thumps me on the back. 'Well, that's no way to answer the question.'

I look him in the eye. 'At first, I thought I'd rather tear that baby with my own hands than let it destroy Lily. But a baby is a miracle, BJ. And if Lily wanted it, even if it killed me, I'd support her. I'd do whatever it took to ensure that she got the best holistic support. I'd have the best doctors in the world waiting in the wings, weeks in advance, to pull that baby out of her.'

'Ah yes, pain is inevitable. Suffering is optional. Smile through da pain.'

'You've got to get your shit together man. Layla needs you like never before.'

'Never in a million years did I ever think I would be in this situation. I feel like a mastodon dying from hundreds of crude spears in my flesh.'

'Come on. Let's get you back.'

He stands and sways slightly before righting himself against the wall of the cave, then turns to go.

'BJ,' I call.

He turns to face me. He's so broken. He looks nothing like the great fighter I once faced. At that moment I realize that he might not be able to survive without Layla. I had been wrong about him. He truly loves my sister.

'I'm sorry I made you have the commitment ceremony,' I say.

'I didn't do it for you.'

He picks up the lamp and starts moving into the dark passage. With a sigh, I follow him.

THIRTY-EIGHT

Layla

Maddie asks me to lunch and we arrange to meet in an Italian restaurant half-way between both our workplaces. I arrive first and am sitting with a bottle of mineral water when she walks through the door. She does not smile when her eyes meet mine. Not even as she slips into the chair opposite me.

'How are you?' she asks.

'I'm fine,' I say, surprised by her unfriendly demeanor.

'Yeah?' Her jaw is clenched, and her tone is an inch away from downright hostility.

I don't react to it. 'Yeah. I'm all right. I'm not in pain or anything like that.'

'Really?'

'Yes, really,' I say, knowing that she is brewing towards some kind of confrontation.

'Well, you're the lucky one, then. Because I'm in pain, and I bet you've got poor BJ bleeding his heart out.'

I stare at her in astonishment.

Her eyes stab at me angrily. 'I never thought I'd say this but you're so cruel, Layla. How could you do this to all of us?' She takes a shuddering breath before carrying on. 'We love you so much, and there you are giving it all up for a ... a ... fucking fetus. It doesn't love you like we do. Fuck, it doesn't even feel.'

I sense myself start to crumble inside. My defenses are weak. Everyday I am fighting to keep it all together when all I want to do is weep. Because I'm the one who could lose everything.

Blindly, I reach for a packet of breadsticks and tear it open. All around us are the civilized, muted sounds of cutlery against plates, conversation, laughter, and piped music.

Don't cry, Layla. Just don't do it.

I pull a stick out and bring it to my mouth, but my body doesn't want it. One part of me says it is full of preservatives another part simply feels too sad to even pretend to eat. No one truly understands. Not Ma, not Jake, not BJ, and now, not even Maddie. Tears are stinging at the backs of my eyes. I blink them away, and place the breadstick back on the pristine tablecloth so it is almost perfectly aligned with the knife.

'Cruel,' I whisper, my eyes fixed on the knife.

'Yes, cruel,' Maddie repeats vehemently. Her voice is strong, indignant, and throbbing with moral righteousness.

I raise my eyes. 'I'm not cruel, Maddie. You know what is cruel? This world is cruel. Fate is cruel. The God that decided that I should have a malignant cancer growing in my womb at the same time as my baby is cruel. And I'll tell you what else is cruel. Asking me to kill my own baby is cruel.'

But Maddie is unmoved. 'We all have to make horrible decisions. Our politicians kill hundreds of totally innocent people everyday in the Middle East and just call it collateral damage. A fetus is not even a proper person,' she cries passionately.

'Is it right? Shall I do it just because they do it?'

'No.' She stops a moment to change tack. 'Doesn't your great love for BJ count for more than this unborn fetus?'

'Love is love. You don't understand. It's the little and unimportant things that give a person away. They call it the waitress test. You can always tell a person by the way he or she treats a waitress. And that's because the waitress stands for someone who has no future value to you. If I claim to love this baby, then what I do to it will ultimately decide how I will love and treat BJ. How much I will be willing to sacrifice for him if he needed me to?'

'I don't want you to die,' she wails suddenly, her eyes suddenly brimming with tears.

'Oh Maddie,' I sigh, and reach out for her hand. Her hand is cold and limp. I grasp it strongly. 'This is not a death sentence. I am taking a calculated risk. Something we take everyday without knowing we are. I could get struck by lightning while I am sleeping in my bed, or get run over while I am crossing the road, or get shot while I am in a cinema by a man who is drugged up to his eyeballs with psychotic drugs.'

Maddie sniffs but she is listening intently to me.

'It may sound like I am being careless, but I am not. I promise you, I'm not. I am going by the findings of the Nobel prize winner, Sir MacFarlene Burnet, who said cancer cells are not foreign bodies. They are defective, mutated cells produced in the hundreds by our bodies. In a normal immune system they are naturally and quickly destroyed. The problem arises when our immune system is compromised, and does not trigger an attack on these rogue cells. So a tumor is not a problem, but a symptom of a failing immune system.'

I take a deep breath. This explanation is as important for me as it is for her.

'Therefore, I'm going to the source of problem. I am going to fix my immune system so it will do the job that it is designed to do. I truly believe the body has powerful healing abilities of its own.'

I gently stroke Maddie's hand and smile sadly at her. 'I love you Maddie. Always.'

Tears start flowing from her eyes. She doesn't attempt to wipe them away.

'Besides Maddie, you know me, I won't roll over and let anybody tell me that this is how it is, and I can never change it. The statistics are clear. Less people die of cancer than of cancer treatments.'

'I was so sad, I could not sleep last night, Layla.'

I bite my lip trying to think of something I can say to make it better. 'Remember that time when we were kids and that really good-looking guy, what's his name again? Oh yes, Marcus, invited us to that party?'

She frowns. 'Yeah.'

'Remember you wanted to go.'

'Yeah.'

'And I didn't because my gut told me something was wrong.'

'And you were right because that party got raided and all those kids got into big trouble,' she finished slowly,

'That same instinct is telling me now to stay away from the doctor's office.'

A new look of understanding comes into Maddie's kind, dear face.

THIRTY-NINE

Layla

I look at the calendar and smile with satisfaction. I have made it to four and a half months. There are only 40 days left. The baby's heartbeat is strong, my skin is glowing, and I have more energy than I have ever had.

At times like this, I feel as if everything happens for a reason. Because this happened to me, Jake bought an organic farm and now the whole family has organic vegetables all year round.

My mother and I have learned so much about things we would never have thought to even think about. We no longer eat wheat or processed foods or anything with preservatives in it. At first it was difficult. But my mother is a culinary genius. Now she even makes ice cream using organic ingredients.

I take out the marijuana leaves that have been soaking for five minutes in water, and put them into the centrifugal juicer and switch it on. For the fifth time today I drink the concoction. I follow it with a spoonful of organic bicarbonate soda mixed in with maple syrup. It is Nora's day off and I am cooking. It's nearly time for BJ to return.

Ever since that night Jake found him in the caves and drove him home he is a completely different man. I remember I went out into the living room to meet him when I heard the car and I saw him stumble like a drunk over the threshold. But when he saw me, he took me in his arms and, as sober as a judge said, 'I love you, Layla. Use me as the rock you lean on.'

After that he was unshakeable in his support. He did everything in his power to assist me, care for me and protect me. Sometimes though, I'd catch him looking at me with a yearning expression. Then he would smile almost sadly and say,

'Sometimes I can't believe how beautiful you are.'

I have a surprise for him today. He insists on eating the same food as me, but today I have brought him a lovely steak from a grass-fed, free-range cow. I called Bertie earlier and she gave me his favorite recipe. 'Make sure you put a knob of butter at the very end. It gives a beautiful rich taste to the meat.'

When I hear his car drive up, I heat the skillet and add a drop of oil. I drain the water from the potatoes and begin to mash them. I lay the meat on the hot metal. The sizzle is terrific. I add butter and milk and lightly mix them into the mashed potatoes as BJ walks through the door.

'Wow! Something smells good,' BJ says coming towards me. He nuzzles my neck. 'And that's not even taking the steak into the mix.'

I laugh.

'So what's with the steak?'

'It's for you,' I say simply.

'I told you. We're both eating the same food.'

'Just this once. I've gone to all the trouble.' I untangle myself from his arms, go to turn the meat and drop in some crushed garlic in the potatoes.

He watches me with folded arms.

'Go on. Sit down.' He sits at the table. It's set with salad and his drink. He takes a sip. I put the knob of butter into the pan and

shake it slightly. My mouth actually begins to water. I haven't had meat in so long. I pull the pan off the fire to let the meat rest and begin to plate up. The mashed potatoes go underneath, with the sliced steak resting on top. I carry the plate to the table and put it in front of BJ.

I sit next to him. '*Bon appetito.*'

He watches me pick up my fork and dip it into my salad of greens, sprouts, seeds, avocado, and tomatoes. Then he sets half his meat onto my plate.

I look up at him. I am so tempted. I can smell it and my stomach is growling. 'I'm not really supposed to,' I say.

'It's just a tiny bit. It won't hurt you. You can have an extra helping of vitamin C or whatever tonight.'

I smile. 'OK. It is grass fed and organic. So it can't be that bad.'

We both cut a piece of meat and put it into our mouths at the same time. It melts in my mouth.

'This,' BJ says, 'is the most delicious piece of meat I have ever tasted. Other than your pussy, of course.'

I laugh, but he is right. We savor it slowly. Afterwards, we walk into the forest. In late summer it is cool and beautiful. It is quiet now, but in the bushes and undergrowth there are badgers and foxes and deer. We follow the little path towards the clearing where BJ's gardener has made a gazebo that he has covered with climbing roses. At this time of the year the roses are on their last showing. The area around it is full of petals giving off the last of their dying scent. We enter the gazebo and sit down.

It is so peaceful. For a long time we say nothing.

But there is something I want to confront him with. Something I must make BJ face. Ever since we found out about the cancer, BJ has never touched my stomach. Even when we are making love, he will avoid touching my belly. I unbutton my shirt from the bottom up and taking his hand, guide it towards my exposed belly. I feel the resistance and rigidity of his hand and look up to him beseechingly.

'Please,'

He relents and allows me to put his hand on my stomach. On contact his eyes darken. We stare into each other's eyes. Kick, Tommy, kick, I pray. There is no one else in the world but he and I. And then a kick. A hard one. We both feel it. Someone else has just entered into our world. We smile at each other. Our eyes filled with wonder.

'He's saying hello,' I say.

'Oh God!' BJ mutters suddenly.

'That's our Tommy,' I say.

'That's our Tommy,' BJ repeats, his voice choked with emotion.

He pulls the edges of my shirt across the bulge of my stomach and carefully drags the buttons through the holes.

 303

'Come on, Princess. Let's get you and little fella home.

FORTY

Layla

"Life should be lived to the point of tears."
—Albert Camus

There are only 20 days left on my calendar. It's still dark as I descend the villa's staircase, holding on to the rough, tree trunk banisters. I cross the beautifully decorated space. It has a stunningly sculpted dining table, giant seashells hanging from the ceiling, a simple but elegant arrangement of tiles and stones and wood seals on the open windows. Soundless on my bare feet I make for the sliding doors. This is a holiday villa in Tulum, Mexico that BJ has brought me to. It used to belong to the drug lord, Pablo Escobar.

'Why Mexico?' I asked excitedly in the plane.

'It's a surprise,' he said with a smile.

And at midnight I found out. He had hired people to hang strings of blue lanterns all over the beach and a Mariachi band to play. There was a jug of non-alcoholic Margaritas on a mat on the beach.

'Don't you recognize it?' he asked.

And it hit me then. Of course, he was making my favorite song come alive. Drinking Margaritas by a string of blue lights under the Mexican sky while listening to the Mariachi playing at midnight. *Are you with me?*

I cried then.

As I walk on the white sand it flows up through my toes. I stand at the water's edge holding my belly. 'Look where we are, Tommy.' The cool morning breeze blows my hair from my face. I let the water rush up my toes and blanket my feet. It is incredibly sensuous. I am still standing there with my eyes closed when BJ comes to stand next to me. I look up at him. His eyebrows are drawn in a straight line making his face full of dark pools of shadow.

'You looked like a mermaid from the window. Something so beautiful I couldn't fathom touching,' he says softly.

I smile at him. 'Come and sit with me. It's so peaceful here.'

We walk away from the water's edge, sit on the white sand, and in perfect silence watch the sunrise together. Things are so different now. Every minute we spend together is like a precious gift. We were among the living. We had to do this. So we did it.

Red. Orange. Yellow. The sky becomes an amazing kaleidoscope of color. Next to us, there is a discarded Coke can. That, too, is life. I turn towards BJ. His face is golden, some shades of red.

'I love you, BJ.'

He leans down as if he wants to see who I am and looks deeply into my eyes.

'What is it?' I ask him.

'I was remembering that first night I found you in my bedroom.'

I grin. 'When you spanked me?'

'When you became wet?'

'You never told me. Were you hard?'

'Like a fucking rock.'

I laugh. 'Why did you come up to your room?'

'I followed you. I saw you go up with Ria. When you didn't come down, I knew that you must have found my bedroom.'

'What did you think when you saw me?'

'When I saw you stealing my tiepin?'

'Mmmm.'

'I could not believe my eyes. Layla Eden in my bedroom. And taking what didn't belong to her. All my Christmases rolled up into one.'

I shrug nonchalantly. 'I wasn't really stealing. It was mine. It had my name on it. Just like you have it across your dick.'

He laughs. 'It's fucking branded on.'

I pick up a handful of sand and let it flow through my fingers.

'Sometimes I wonder what would have happened if Ria had not asked me to use the upstairs bathroom. Would we never have got together?'

He takes my hand in his. His touch is soothing. 'I always dreamed of what it would be like to be with you. We didn't hook up by accident. I was always looking for a way to make you notice me. You had me from the day you lifted your skirt and showed me your polka dot panties.'

'I didn't lift it and show it to you,' I protest indignantly. 'I fell down.'

'That's what they all say.'

'Oh you are big-headed.'

'That's what they all say.'

'Oh!' I slap him around the head and he pushes me on the sand. The sex is gentle. The sea. The sand. The orange sky. They were all witnesses. They would keep the memory of my love for this man if by chance

I am not able. Inside my belly, Tommy kicks lustily.

Take care of Daddy, if I am not around.

FORTY-ONE

BJ

I buy her flowers and watch her stroke them as if they are hurt children she is soothing. Since that night in the caves with Jake, I don't tell her anymore how much everyday hurts. She is dying right before my eyes and there is not one damn thing I can do about it. I want to bellow. I want to howl. But it would frighten her. She looks at the calendar with joy. She is another day closer to her goal. I look at it with terror. I am another day to closer to finding out how much of her the cancer has eaten.

How much is left.

She hides things from me. I know she has written letters for Tommy. Eighteen. To be given to him on his birthdays. She gave them to her mother. I accidentally overheard her conversation. The intolerable pain of that discovery is impossible to describe. I wanted to go and fight ten men. I wanted to hurt someone the way I was hurting. I went into the bathroom and made a hole in the wall. It hurt like a mother. But it dulled the other pain.

Sometimes, when I have to share her with her family, I feel resentful. I feel as if they are stealing my time. What little is left.

I don't know how much more I can take of any of these feelings.

Everyday she makes me touch her belly. But I don't know how I feel about Tommy. He's my flesh and blood. He's mine and there is a connection, but there is no love in my heart. There is no place for him. For me there is only Layla.

I cannot love anyone else.

Not now.

Not yet.

Maybe because my heart has been ripped open and I'm bleeding. Maybe that's it.

After that night at Heat Exchange, I've never gone to a club or a strip joint. We entered the VIP room. She got out of her little dress, opened her legs wide, showed me her pussy, and asked if I wanted to touch

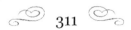

it outside of work, and I felt nothing. Just disgust at myself. My dick was limp. I paid her and left. I knew when I walked out of that door that I had gone to the wrong place. What I was looking for could not be found in a bar or a strip club. Instead I retreated to a place where I'd found solace in the past. Somewhere I could not be found. In the darkness of the old smugglers' caves.

Bob Marley is singing, *No Woman No Cry*. The calendar reads Ten Days More. And oh yeah, its got a drawing of a happy face next to it.

FORTY-TWO

Layla

Tomorrow is the big day. Because I opted out of a biopsy that could cause me to miscarry, it will be like opening Pandora's box. They will do a biopsy on everything in my uterus to assess how bad the situation is. Immediately after, they will operate to remove the baby and perform the hysterectomy.

They don't know how long I will be out. The cesarean will only take 45 to 60 minutes. It's what needs doing after that's the unknown factor. I think I am too numb to feel afraid.

My bag is packed. It is an optimistic bag. There is chewing gum to help speed the process of bowel function returning to normal after a cesarean birth, compression stockings, sanitary towels, and a pair of champagne glasses.

How strange, then, that it feels as if I am packing never to return.

We have a quiet dinner early, as I am not allowed to eat after 8pm. I eat lightly and BJ doesn't eat at all. We talk a little. We stare at each other a lot. As if we are never going to see each other again. We end up in the bedroom. That afternoon I had taken the time to scent the place with aromatherapy oils, scented candles, and made the bed with silk sheets that I ordered from the Internet. By the bed there was tray of fruit and a big beautiful box of chocolates.

'Do you know?' he whispers to me. 'The sexual texts from The Ming dynasty regarded a woman's sexual organs as a crucible or a stove from which a man could cultivate vitality.'

'Oh, yeah,' I say biting my lower lip.

'Yeah. Want to try something Ming?' For a moment the old BJ glitters in the candlelight. Tonight he is strong and powerful and I am putty in his hands.

'OK.'

'Get totally naked, then shake your whole body; your legs, your head, and your sweet ass. Afterwards, sit down cross-legged on the bed and invite me into your body.'

So I shake my entire body, sit down, and ask him to come into me. He takes off his clothes, muscles rippling across every part of his body, and his cock standing to attention like a good soldier. He comes to sit in front of me.

'When I exhale, you inhale and vice versa. Pretend that you are able to take that breath you inhaled from me down to your sex organs.'

As he breathes out, I find myself breathing his breath into my body and down to my sex. Up so close he nearly takes my breath away. He is such a magnificent specimen.

Slowly, I become conscious that I am sharing all of me with him and he is doing the same. The realization makes my skin super sensitive, as if an electric current is running through my body.

He stares into my eyes. 'Now kiss me and share your breath with me.'

So we kiss and kiss and kiss and the strangest thing happens. I don't believe woo-woo stuff but suddenly, amongst the

scent of the candles and aromatherapy oils and the silk sheet under us, we become one person. And I'm not even talking about BJ and I. I'm talking about BJ, Tommy, and I. Suddenly we are joined in a kind of magic circle. All of us linked forever. No matter what happens after tonight, we will always be together.

And then I am back in my physical body, on my hands and knees, reveling in the muscular caress of his shaft. He is like he was in the old days, before the cancer. Raw and unbelievably passionate. I feel his large hands on my body. Touching, claiming, branding. It is as it was on our very first night.

The orgasm when it comes is so shattering, so incredible, so crazy I can't even scream.

'Wow! That was so ... mind blowing,' I pant breathlessly.

He turns his raven eyes to me. 'You're mind blowing.'

'So are you going to honey talk me now?' I tease with a smile

'Why not? You are everything I could have dreamed of. You're a cool, cool girl, Layla.'

I look into his beautiful eyes. How I love this man. I take his warm, rough hands in my own. 'No matter what happens tomorrow, you know, I'll always love you.'

Something sad and dark crosses his face, but he hides it as quickly as it showed itself.

'Are you ready for your goodnight kiss?' he asks lightly.

As he has done from the day we got married, he opens my legs and lingeringly kisses me right in the middle of my sex.

'Good night, my darling,' he whispers softly into my core.

"Jump into the angry abyss with a smile on
your face.
This how magic has always been created."
—Shamans

FORTY-THREE

BJ

Her eyes look like they are lit up from within and her skin is actually glowing. I remember something that scares me out of my wits. My grandmother once told me that a few hours before death the person always glows. You think they are getting better, but they are really just preparing for the final journey.

We are at the hospital. Her family is gathered outside. They have said their well wishes and now it's my turn. Only I can't say anything. I am too afraid I will break down.

I can feel my insides sloshing hotly. I have never been so frightened in all my life.

'You will tell Tommy that I love him and I always will,' she says. There is slight tremor to her voice and fear in her eyes. She is just as terrified as I am.

Fuck, I can't do this. 'Fucking tell him yourself,' I say.

'Say something nice to me,' she says softly.

But I can't. If I stop being a son of a bitch I'm going to howl my eyes out. 'When you get out of here, I'm gonna fuck you so hard you're gonna need stitches.'

'I said say something nice.'

'It's hard to say something nice when you are bleeding out.'

'Oh darling.'

The nurse comes in. 'It's time,' she says.

I grab Layla's hand.

'Don't be afraid,' she whispers. 'I'm not.'

I want to cry. I want to envelop her in my arms and not let them take her away, but I let go of her hand and watch them wheel her through the swing doors. I stand there, lost and frightened in the empty room. I am so fucking frightened my breath comes out in a huge heave through my body. I feel a hand touch me. I turn around

'Come with me,' Jake says. His voice is firm and authoritative. And like a lost child I follow him outside. I feel hollow and

emasculated. I let her go. She could die on the operating table.

I should have told her that she is one in a billion.

EPILOGUE

BJ

"Not to dream boldly may turn out to be
irresponsible"

—George Leonard

There are fresh flowers on the grave. My
mother must have visited earlier. I stand by
the headstone and I feel a sense of serenity.
For the first time in my life I feel at peace.
There is no hate, no anger, no pain, no hurt.

All the lost jigsaw pieces of my life
have come together in a brilliantly beautiful

mosaic. Only now, I can see why that red piece happened, or why that blackness had to be right there, where I thought it should not be.

Now I see how perfect it all is.

There is a small ladybug on the black marble of my father's gravestone. I get down on my haunches and watch it. A gust of wind comes and it flies away. I touch the stone. It is warm from the morning sun.

I never thought the day would come when I would forgive my father. It reminds me of what a man once told me. He was a heroin addict.

'I am not to be reviled. I'm to be pitied. You have to walk in a man's shoes before you judge him,' he said.

I didn't understand him then, but I do now. I know that given the right circumstances, I could have been my father. Maybe I wouldn't have battered Tommy, but I wouldn't have loved him. Without Layla, I would have been dead inside the way my father was.

He was not to be reviled, he was to be pitied.

I turn away from the grave and walk towards the car. I have to stop by the local store and get a carton of organic milk for Layla. I haven't told you what happened, have I? They wheeled her into the operating theater to do the biopsy, only to find no tumor during the ultrasound. It had shrunk to nothing. They couldn't believe it. They probably still can't. They didn't even have to perform a Cesarean. Layla had been right all along. She never stopped believing. She made the miracle happen.

Layla carried our baby to full term.

Tommy was born a healthy, lusty baby weighing 8lb and 2 ounces. A bundle of joy.

It's a beautiful day, so I park the car and walk down the road to the corner shop.

'Coming for your milk, Mr. Pilkington?' Mr. Singh calls.

'Yup,' I say picking up a carton.

'Tell your wife, organic yogurt coming next week.'

I grin. 'That'll make her day.'

'Yes, yes, your wife very interested in organic things. She always looking for seeds. I tell her, I bring from India for her.'

'Thanks, Mr. Singh.'

'No problem.'

The bell jangles when I close the door. I light a cigarette and smoke it on the walk home. I kill it outside the front steps and chuck it into the bushes. I fit the key into the lock, open the door, and step inside.

Layla is coming down the stairs. She breaks into a smile.

'Hey,' she calls gaily and runs down the rest of the way.

I watch her approach, a sunburst in my heart. 'You look good enough to eat.'

'Never mind that now. I've got a secret to tell you,' she whispers.

'What is it?' I ask.

She giggles. 'It involves adding to the world's overpopulation problem.'

My eyes widen. I feel ten feet tall. I put the bag of milk on the floor and move closer. She smells of milk and baby powder. She starts laughing as I pick her up by her waist and whisk her into the air and whirl her. Round and round we go until we are both dizzy.

'You made me dizzy,' she says laughing.

Love is just a word until someone comes along and gives it meaning.

She. She is the meaning.

-The End –

This book is dedicated to
Gianna Beretta Molla.
Took the same decision as Layla, but did not
survive.
Gianna was canonized as a saint of the
Roman Catholic Church in 2004.

"Lord, keep your grace in my heart. Live in
me so your grace be mine.
Make that I may bear everyday some flowers
and new fruit."
Gianna Beretta Molla, 1922-1962

If you enjoyed Sexy Beast and want to know
how Jake met Lily you'll find it here:

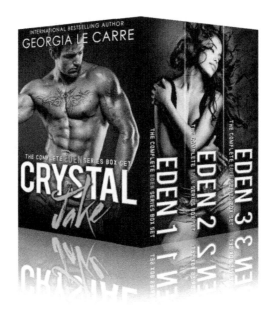

Amazon US:
http://www.amazon.com/dp/B00X2JUCRC
Amazon
UK: http://www.amazon.co.uk/gp/product/B0
0X2JUCRC

Canada: http://www.amazon.ca/gp/product/
B00X2JUCRC
Amazon Aus:
http://www.amazon.com.au/gp/product/B00
X2JUCRC

I **LOVE** hearing from my readers so by all means come and say hello here: https://www.facebook.com/georgia.lecarre

or

Click on the link below to receive news of my latest releases, great giveaways, and exclusive content.
http://bit.ly/10e9WdE

On another note... :-)

Want To Help An Author?

Please leave a review. Reviews help other readers find an author's work. No matter how short it may be, it is very *precious*. *Links for your Amazon store below.*

Thank you!

http://www.amazon.com/dp/B01 2GRLQJI

http://www.amazon.co.uk/dp/B012GRLQJI

http://www.amazon.com.au/gp/product/B012GRLQJI

http://www.amazon.ca/gp/product/B012GRLQJI

GOLD DIGGER

Georgia Le Carre

CHAPTER 1

'**W**hatever you do, don't *ever* trust them. Not one of them,' he whispered. His voice was so feeble I had to strain to catch it.

'I won't,' I said, softly.

'They are dangerous in a way you will never understand. Never let your guard down,' he insisted.

'I understand,' I said, but all I wanted was for him to stop talking about them. These last precious minutes I didn't want to waste on them.

He shook his head unhappily. 'No, no, you don't understand. You can never let your guard down for even an instant. Never.'

'All right, I won't.'

'I will be a very sad spirit if you do.'

'I won't,' I promised vehemently, and reached for his hand. The contrast between my hand and his couldn't have been greater. Mine was smooth and soft and his was gnarled and full of green veins, the skin waxy and liver-spotted. The nails were the color of polished ivory. The hand of a seventy-year-old man. His fingers grasped fiercely at my hand. I lifted them to my lips and kissed them one by one, tenderly.

His eyes glowed briefly in his wasted, sunken face. 'How I love you, my darling Tawny,' he murmured.

'I love you. I love you. I love you,' I said.

'Do your part and they cannot touch you.'

He sighed. 'It's nearly time.'

'Don't say that,' I cried, even though I knew in my heart that he was right.

His eyes swung to the window. 'Ah,' he sighed softly. 'You've come.'

My gaze chased his. The window he was looking at was closed, the heavy drapes pulled shut. Goose pimples crawled up my arms. 'Don't go yet. Please,' I begged.

He dragged his gaze reluctantly from the window. His thin, pale lips rose at the edges as he drew in a rattling breath. 'I've got to go, my darling. I've got to pay my dues. I haven't been a good man.'

'Just wait a while.'

'You have your whole life ahead of you.'

He turned his unnaturally bright eyes away from me, looked straight ahead, and with a violent shudder, departed.

For a few seconds I simply stared at him. Appropriately, outside the October wind howled and dashed itself into the shutters. I knew the servants were waiting downstairs. Everyone was waiting for me to go down and tell them the news. Then I leaned forward and put my cheek on his still, bony chest. He smelled strongly of medicine. I closed my eyes tightly. Why did you have to go and die and leave me to the wolves?

In that moment I felt so close to him I wished that this time would not end. I wished I could lie on his chest, safe and

closeted away from the cruel world. I heard the clock ticking. The flames in the fireplace crackled and spat. Somewhere a pipe creaked. I placed my chin on his chest and turned to look at him one last time. He appeared to be sleeping. Peaceful at any rate. I stroked the thin strands of white hair lying across his pinkish white scalp, and let my finger run down his prominent nose. It shocked me how quickly the tip of his nose had lost warmth. Soon all of him would be stone cold.

I wondered whom he had seen at the window. Who had come to take him to his reckoning. My sorrow was complete. I could put my fingertips into it and feel the edges. Smooth. Without corners. Without sharpness. It had no tears. I knew he was dying two hours before. Strange because it had seemed as if he had taken a turn for the better. He seemed stronger, his cheeks pink, his eyes brilliantly bright and when he smiled it appeared as if he was lit from within. He even looked so much stronger. I asked him what he wanted to eat.

'Milk. I'll have a glass of milk,' he said decisively.

But after I called for milk and it was brought to him he smiled and refused it. 'Isn't this wonderful?' he asked. 'I feel so good.'

And at that moment I knew. Even so it was incomprehensible to me that he was really gone. I never wanted to believe it.

 333

'In the end you wanted to go, didn't you?'

There was no answer.

'It's OK. I know you were tired. It was only me holding you back. You go on ahead. Find a place for me.'

He lay as still as a corpse. Oh God! I already missed him so much.

'I understand you can't talk. But you can hear me. When it is my turn I want you to come and get me. I'll be expecting you to come in through the window. Go in peace now, my love. All will be well. They will never know the truth. I will never tell them. To the day you come back to collect me.'

And then I began to cry, not loud, ugly sobs, but a quiet weeping. I didn't want the servants to hear. To come rushing in. Call the doctor waiting downstairs to come in and pronounce him dead. I knew what waited for me outside this room. Another hour...or two wouldn't make a difference. This was my time. My final hours with my husband.

The time before I became the hated gold digger.

Printed in Great Britain
by Amazon

25484028R00192